MW01528147

R _ 95

Selkie

FROM THE LIBRARY OF

Also by Anne Cameron

Fiction
The Whole Fam Damily
A Whole Brass Band
Escape to Beulah
Deejay & Betty
Kick the Can
Bright's Crossing
Women, Kids & Huckleberry Wine
South of an Unnamed Creek
Stubby Amberchuk and the Holy Grail

Traditional Tales
Tales of the Cairds
Dzelarhons

Poems
The Annie Poems
Earth Witch

Stories for Children
The Gumboot Geese
Raven Goes Berrypicking
Raven and Snipe
Spider Woman
Lazy Boy
Orca's Song
Raven Returns the Water
How the Loon Lost her Voice
How Raven Freed the Moon

Stories on Cassette (Audio Book)
Loon and Raven Tales

anne ◆ cameron

Selkie

HARBOUR PUBLISHING

Copyright © 1996 by Anne Cameron

All rights reserved. The use of any part of this publication reproduced, transmitted in any form or by any means, electronic, mechanical, photocopying, recording, or otherwise, or stored in a retrieval system, without the prior consent of the publisher is an infringement of the copyright law.

Harbour Publishing
P.O. Box 219
Madeira Park, BC Canada V0N 2H0

Published with the assistance of the Canada Council and the Government of British Columbia, Cultural Services Branch.

Cover illustration by Gaye Hammond
Cover design and page composition by Martin Nichols
Typeset in Cheltenham Light
Printed and bound in Canada

Canadian Cataloguing in Publication Data

Cameron, Anne, 1938-
  Selkie

  ISBN 1-55017-152-6

  I. Title.
PS8555.A5187S44 1996 C813'.54   C96-910488-X
PR9199.3.C2775S44 1996

Selkie

Selkies, Silkies or Sealkies were originally seals. They are capable of leaving their seal skins behind and walking on the earth as women or men. They often live with or marry humans, and have even been recorded as having children. Selkies are beautiful, with soft, lovely hair. Unfortunately, their children have a tendency toward pointed, carnivore-like teeth, and seem overly fond of the taste of raw fish or fresh blood. There are many stories of selkies falling in love with humans and bringing great fortune with them, but somehow the people always seem to ruin things.

— *Tales of the Cairds* —

– I –

Cassidy Forbes was asleep when it started to rain.

She was deep into a dream which was so familiar to her, she was almost more at home in it than in her regular waking world. She'd been through the awful part of it, the part where she was running, running, hiding, trying so hard to flee that the horror of it was almost more than she could bear. Her frustration would escalate in that part of the dream, and her fear. She'd be running, her lungs burning, the stitch in her side threatening to freeze her in her tracks, and then she'd see a car and get in it and somehow manage to hot-wire it. Off she'd go in the car, her relief enormous, and just about the time the terror was gone, the car would begin to slow down. No matter what Cassidy did in her dream, the car went slower and slower until she was almost pushing it. Finally, knowing the threat was gaining again, Cassidy would get out of the car and start to run, but the ground would turn to molasses, she'd have to drag each foot out of the sticking goo and it would take all her strength to go one step. To add to the fun, roots caught at her ankles and tree branches grabbed at her head, and she knew these were obstacles only for her, not for the threat that chased her. Just before the threat got her—and waking or sleeping Cassidy knew full well the threat was her

7

father—Cassidy would get past the horrible part to this part, the safe-at-last part.

It was a house, a house she knew she had never seen, not in waking life anyway. The house was enormous and most of it was pretty much toast, but the central section was just fine. Cassidy became familiar with this part of the house, so familiar with it she felt more at home there than in her regular waking house. A nice kitchen, old-fashioned and welcoming, with the kind of glass-fronted unpainted wooden cabinets everyone used to have but now you only see them in Harrowsmith, and a big old porcelain sink with a porcelain drainboard, angled slightly downward and ridged like an old scrubbing board. The kitchen table was plain blond wood, unpainted but Danish-oiled to a soft sheen, and the chairs were the kind that came high up your back, so comfortable you could spend the rest of your life sitting in them.

The kitchen had a door leading to the outside, and another door leading to a hallway. At the end of the hallway was a bathroom with a huge claw-footed tub and a pedestal hand basin. The towel racks were the same white porcelain as the tub and basin and the toilet was by itself in a small attached room, which Cassidy thought was just about the most civilized thing in the world.

One room had a single bed, a small couch which could be jiggered around so it would fold out into another single bed, a round table in front of a window which sometimes looked out on the sea, at other times looked out on an orchard. There were two chairs at this table, and on the table-top a box of very nice paper, a fountain pen and a little blue bottle of ink with a rubber stopper in it. The bureau and drawers were blond wood, and on the floor was a braided rug. In an adjoining room was a huge rolltop desk, a piano, a music stand, some comfortable chairs, walls of books and a positively glorious piece of furniture, something like a sideboard but not quite. Cassidy wasn't sure what it was for because each time she reached out to open it, the scene changed and she wasn't in that room any more. A few experiences like that and she learned that as long as she didn't attempt to open that piece of furniture, she could stay in that room. There she could read, or look out the window, or write, or even play the piano, which was wonderful because in this other place people insist on calling reality, Cassidy couldn't play anything except the radio or the TV.

What she loved most about the house was the way you'd find these hidden rooms. A couple of them she could find each and every time the dream came to her, rooms hidden off the walls of the stairwell leading to the next floor. If you knew where to look, you could find a part of the wall which opened, like a door, and when you stepped through the doorway into what you thought would be the wall—pow! You were in a whole other part of the house. Mostly bedrooms, but in one room there was a small stove, a small table and a little Minnie Mouse-sized sink ideal for one person. This room wasn't exactly a kitchen, but it could be used as one. It wasn't any particular kind of room at all, yet it was next to every kind of room a person could want. When you looked out the window above the little sink, there was the same view you could see from the downstairs kitchen. And yet when you stood outside and looked at the house, you saw the downstairs kitchen and above it the roofline, as if the second floor didn't go all the way the width of the house.

There were other hidden rooms, in each one of them gorgeous old furniture, the kind Cassidy coveted, the kind she would have stolen if she'd known where to go to steal it. In one room, another library, was a brass vase. Or maybe it was what Cassidy's grandmother had referred to as a "jardineer." Cassidy was pretty sure Gran had meant "jardiniere" but you didn't argue with Gran then, so why start now. Too big to be sat on a table of any kind, the brass vase-jardineer stood on the floor, and only sometimes had dried reeds or grasses been arranged in it. Four enormous dragons lived on the sides of the brass vase, their tails, legs and claws intertwining. The whole effect was somehow very Chinese, but asleep or awake, Cassidy knew there was nothing Chinese about any of it. The vase and the dragons were Celtic, and the vase might not be brass at all, but bronze, and so old, so very old.

Other hidden rooms were practically falling off of or out of the house. Some of them gaped empty, with holes in the floors or walls, birds nesting in the ceiling and flying out the hollow places where there had once been windows, or flitting up and down long unused chimneys.

Sometimes it seemed as if there were other people here, although Cassidy had never seen them, just heard them or caught a glimpse of a shadow. She never had to hide from them. But even in the house the threat would make itself known. The air would get cold and press down on her, heavier and heavier and heavier. That's when she would start up the stairs, find the place, step through the door into the hidden section of the house. There was a bar there, like a common two-by-four except double-planed on all sides, polished, and just about the most beautiful piece of wood Cassidy had ever seen. She would fit it into two heavy brass or maybe bronze brackets—and the feeling of oppression would vanish. Just like that. Cassidy could then relax, even go to the hidden kitchen and put the little kettle on the gas ring of the tiny stove, make herself a cup of tea and sit at the table-for-two looking out the window at the front yard, or the orchard or the meadows or the rose arbour or whatever was the front yard that time. Often she saw horses out there, placid, big-bodied, strong-legged animals with full manes and tails. Sometimes she saw the threat, but as long as she stayed in the hidden part she was safe. The threat had no idea where she was. She could have opened her hidden kitchen window, leaned out and spat on his head if she had wanted. She preferred to sit quietly at the table, sipping tea and fully enjoying the absence of fear.

But when it started to rain, she wasn't that far along in the dream. She was in the room with the rolltop desk and the treasured piece of furniture she didn't dare open. She wanted to stay there much longer, playing piano and doing anything else she wanted, but there was the rain, and her husband Michael disturbing her. She withdrew unwillingly from her haven.

"Jesus, Cassie, how can you sleep through *this!* Wake up, will you, the pipes have burst or something!"

Cassidy hated being called Cassie, but somewhere about the five-hundredth time she'd told him that and been ignored, she quit protesting. She never introduced herself as Cassie, she always signed Cassidy, and still he persisted. Cassidy had finally decided it was his way of trying to diminish her, to think of her as a child or less than an adult, less than him.

"Cassie, *Jesus*, will you wake *up*. What's wrong with you? Are you *on* something? Get *up* and help me find the problem here!"

Cassidy managed to sit up, she even managed to half focus her eyes, but she couldn't quite come awake, it was almost as if she were still caught in the dream world. The bed was soaked, her nightgown was soaked, the carpet on the floor was soaked, and water came from the ceiling in what you would call a downpour if you were outside and walking in it, or watching it from the window. Cassidy could accept it—rain was supposed to fall from on high—but she was a bit puzzled by the fact that just as much water was pouring sideways from the walls, all four of them.

"Cassie! I can't do it by myself! Now, come *on!*"

So Cassidy swung her two-tons-each legs over the side of the bed and put her feet on the floor. The water came to her ankles, and it was warm. She knew if she just sat there long enough it would be deep enough for her to swim in.

"If you don't get a move on I'm going to drag you! Getting you awake is like getting a wisdom tooth pulled, it can be done but you can't look forward to it." Michael was not only upset at the pipes being frapped, he was furious with her for not being as upset as he was.

Cassie started walking, following him, and it was like that part of the dream where the thick goo held her feet and each movement happened in super-slow motion. But anything was better than Michael's anger, his tongue and his words like whips or little darting swords, pick pick, slash slash, cut cut, hurt hurt hurt hurt.

She took the big emergency flashlight he handed her and went down the cellar stairs behind him, then shone the light so he could see what he was doing when he wrestled with the shut-off valve. He got it turned to Off, wiped his hands on the seat of his sodden pyjamas, then waited, as if he expected the water to stop dripping and spraying from the ceilings and walls. It didn't.

He was past furious to livid with rage, and Cassidy wished she could do or say something to defuse him, but when

Michael got angry the best thing she could do was try hard to become invisible.

"Well, are you going to stand there for the rest of the night like some kind of bump on a log, holding the damn flashlight until the battery goes dead?" he yelled. "Or are you going to go to the goddamn kitchen and make some coffee or something?"

Cassidy turned and headed for the stairs to the kitchen. She made sure to turn the beam so that Michael, coming behind her, could see where he was going. She realized her eyes were wide and almost unblinking, and her face was slack, her lips parted slightly. Anyone looking at her would think she was seriously retarded or in a daze.

Every listing under Plumbers in the phone book got Michael nothing but an answering machine, and that made him angrier. "You'd think they'd take turns, the way doctors take turns covering the Emergency ward at the hospital," he griped. "I suppose if the main water line burst we'd all have to sit in water to our arses waiting for the plumbers to show up for work. They're just servicemen, it's not as if we were talking professionals here, all a person has to know to be a plumber is water runs downhill, you can't get a four-inch turd through a three-inch pipe and payday is on Friday." He almost threw the phone across the kitchen, then yelled at Cassidy. "Well, aren't you going to at least *wake up?* The damn kettle is boiling itself dry, Cassie, maybe you could *do* something about that?"

She managed to make coffee using the little china pot, the plastic cone and the paper filters. She didn't dare use the electric coffeemaker, because what if the water short-circuited the wires and they both got electrocuted or something? She was almost afraid to open the fridge door for the same reason, but she would rather have been given a jolt and a zap than have Michael pitch a fit because she didn't have the cream out for his coffee.

It hadn't done any good turning the shut-off valve. Rain still fell from the ceiling, water still spurted from the walls, and now it was above her ankles, almost to her calves. Michael was on the phone, yelling at the police, demanding they do something, wake up a plumber, wake up the city inspector, get the water main shut down, *anything*, damn it, before the whole house washed away. Cassidy figured the police were going to arrive any minute, all set to arrest Michael and take him off to the psychiatric ward, and she didn't want to greet the constabulary in a soaking wet, clinging nightgown which undoubtedly revealed every curve, dip and dimple of her body. So she fought herself out of whatever it was had her in its grip. She woke up, walked out of the kitchen and headed upstairs to see if she could find some clothes. Wet or dry, it didn't matter, as long as when the police arrived she didn't look like a contestant in a wet tee shirt competition. Cassidy woke up.

And the rain stopped. The entire house was still sodden, but at least no more water was pouring from the ceiling and the walls. "I *knew* turning the shut-off valve was the right thing to do!" Michael called loudly from downstairs. Cassidy didn't bother answering him. She was hauling on her clothes and thanking all the elder gods and goddesses for the fact the jeans might be a bit damp, but the bra and shirt were dry.

She was drinking coffee when the police arrived. They seemed almost disappointed to find Michael calmed down enough they had no excuse to bash him on the head, put him in handcuffs and take him off to have him committed. They walked around downstairs, then went upstairs, commenting on how the water was draining from the bedroom floors and the hallway in a series of little waterfalls. They had a look around upstairs, but when you've seen one soaking wet room you've seen them all, and because the rain had stopped, they were either unwilling or unable to believe Michael's story of how the place had got soaked.

"Guess you'll have to get a plumber," one of them commented.

"No! Really?" Michael gave him the look he usually reserved for Cassidy, the one that told her she was a big disappointment to him.

She knew the best she could hope for was that she'd only make him impatient, and she practically turned herself inside out to keep him from getting angry. Sometimes she wondered why he'd asked her to marry him and then insisted. Maybe he thought he'd be able to change her, educate her, improve her, even *fix* her. She married him and became the mother of a small child before she found out what he really thought of her and her way of doing things. Just little things at first.

"Why don't you butter the top of the bread when you first take it out of the oven, like my mother does?"

"I didn't know you preferred it that way. I always kind of liked it crustier and—"

"Well, I like it buttered."

So the next time she made bread, she dutifully buttered the tops of the hot loaves. Instead of being satisfied with that, he seemed to take some kind of encouragement. His mother hadn't made the top of her macaroni and cheese crisp the way Cassidy did. He preferred a very mild spaghetti sauce. He wanted his beef cooked until it was brown all the way through. He practically had a fit when she added garlic to just about anything a person would care to name.

Cassidy had always enjoyed food and everyone except Michael had thought her a good cook, but by the time her second daughter was heading off to kindergarten, the meals Cassidy made were as bland and one-same-as-the-other as the ones her mother-in-law cooked.

Michelle, the oldest girl, was in grade three and Corinne, the younger, was in grade one when Michael was promoted to a job which sometimes had him out of town for several days at a time. Without the quality control taste tester, Cassidy started cooking again her way, and found to her delight that the girls, usually distressingly uninterested in eating, sat down and gleefully packed away generous servings of everything. Michelle even asked for seconds.

Nobody had to say anything about it. They knew that when Michael came home they'd be back to the best of British cooking, most of it beige. The more adventurous meals not only filled the belly and warmed the heart, they forged a special bond between Cassidy and her daughters. Eventually Michael came to call it the Cannibal Conspiracy, and claimed they were trying to devour him alive.

Michael was very disappointed that he had no son, and he wanted one. He nagged and pestered Cassidy to have another child, to keep having children until they had a boy— and preferably two or more boys. It wasn't that Cassidy begrudged him the sons he wanted, it was just that somehow she didn't have the same level of interest she'd had at the start. She loved her daughters, she figured two kids were enough, and she just didn't want to go through the whole thing again.

Michael said so many things about only having girls that Cassidy finally got impatient. "It's the father who determines the gender of the baby," she said. That's when he hit her for the first time. No warning at all. Just like her father. Not even a change of expression, just *whap* and she was knocked to the floor.

She didn't yelp or even cry. She didn't ask him, "Why did you do that?" She just got up and went to the kitchen to get some ice to put on her face. There wasn't any ice, so she took out a bag of frozen peas. It would do just as well. But before she put it on her face, she made sure she filled all the ice cube trays with water and put them in to freeze. Better that than have Michael find out they were out of ice.

After that she was coldly determined not to get pregnant. Michael threw away her birth control pills, so she got more. He threw them away too, along with her diaphragm and two tubes of Delfen cream once he had found them. When she went to her doctor to ask to have an IUD inserted he shook his head, his face red, and told her Michael had already phoned him.

"It isn't up to *him!*" she blurted. "*I'm* the one would have to—"

"I think you and Michael should see someone, some neutral party, and talk this out, Cass, and until you and he can agree on something, I'm afraid . . . " He let it trail off, and just as well because Cassidy wasn't even listening to him. She was off her chair and walking toward the door, unable to believe that in this so-called modern day and age, she had no say at all about being an incubator or a brood mare.

Michael was convinced she was hiding something. Pills, or spermicidal cream, or something. He watched her like a hawk. She knew he was going through her drawers looking for whatever it was she was using for birth control, she knew he had practically made a list of everything in the medicine chest. She knew he had even looked in the box of tampons in the cupboard under the basin, in case she'd tried to out-smart him by hiding things there.

Well, he didn't find anything, because there wasn't any-thing to find. Maybe it was the praying did it. Every morning when she got up, she prayed that she was one day closer to her period. Every time Michael put his hands on her and moved her so he could roll on top, she prayed that her cervix would slam shut. Every time he finished with her, she prayed his sperm would perish the instant they dared to invade her body. She even thought of running a "Thank you St. Jude" ad in the paper because month after month, to her intense relief, her period arrived.

The second time Michael hit her was when he suggested that she might have been somehow damaged or injured when Corinne was born, and that maybe she was no longer fertile, and she said, "Maybe it's not me." She knew even before she said it that she'd enrage him, but she said it any-way. And sure enough, *whap*, he let her have a good one on the side of the face. She didn't hit the floor, though, because she had half expected it and was ready for it. She lurched sideways, put out her hand and stopped herself from banging into the wall, then walked into the kitchen for her bag of frozen peas.

The peas helped with the swelling but couldn't do any-thing about the bruising, and at suppertime both girls looked from her face to their father's face, their eyes accusing. Michael flushed. He knew they knew he was responsible for the bruise. He glared at them, daring them silently.

Michelle didn't say anything about the bruise, or about her mother's face or her father's temper. She found a new and unexpected way to get under his skin. She tasted her supper, then looked at her mother and in the sweetest voice imaginable said, "Momma, this meal is as blah and tasteless as that swill Grandmother makes. I don't want to hurt your feelings, but I really don't think I could ram any of this down my throat."

"Me neither," Corinne agreed. "Mikey's right, it's like that cabbagey-tasting pablum Grandmother cooks."

"Eat your supper," Michael snapped.

"May I be excused, please?" Michelle had politeness hanging off her in wads.

"May I leave the table, Momma?" Corinne might have taken a course from Madame Whoozits School of Etiquette, Manners and Charm.

"Yes, dears," Cassidy smiled and she knew they knew she knew what they were up to.

It gave her a hint for the next good battleground. She made two suppers, one for her and the girls, one for Michael. His was cooked exactly the way he said he preferred, theirs was pungent with spices and so loaded with garlic it was practically lifting from the table. The girls started at one side of their plates and worked themselves over to the other side and not one Yum yum or Mmm ever good escaped their simmering father.

It wasn't that Cassidy no longer cared she was a huge disappointment to Michael, it was just that she recognized she couldn't possibly make up for her many inadequacies and failures. So she gave up trying to please him and concentrated instead on making life for the girls as pleasant as possible.

Two or three times a year Michael expected Cassidy to pull together a supper with the boss and his wife, and maybe one or two middle management men and their wives, or to throw a party to which all those he thought he should butter up would be invited. Cassidy practically wore herself to a nub getting everything ready, and it was the one area in their life together which didn't seem to disappoint Michael or leave him staring into space as though listening to a far-away Peggy Lee singing, "Is that all there is?" Cassidy really did bend over backward to make everything as good as it could be. She cooked and cooked some more, she made pâté, she made her own sausage rolls, she made mini-quiches, she made Swedish meatballs. She got the biggest prawns she could find, breaded them, cooked them, then arranged them tails in, bodies fanning out on a bed of lettuce. She made her own version of head cheese, which had no "head" in it but veal, rabbit and chicken, boiled, stripped from the bones, boiled some more, then put through a grinder with plenty of onion and seasonings, boiled again, then left to sit in its own jelly, chilled for several days and sliced thin on slices of Cassidy's homemade sourdough bread.

She made two or three kinds of potato salad, several bean salads, green salads, mixed salads and grated carrot with raisin and apple salads, she made sweet and sour chicken balls and a person wouldn't find one, not one, salad made with gelatin or jello. No green jello with peas in it, no red jello with grated cabbage. If there was any jello at all, it was part of dessert.

And every time, for supper or dinner or an all-out party, Cassidy made Baked Alaska. Never fail, absolutely positively guaranteed, because if there was one thing Cassidy loved, it was Baked Alaska, just because it was such an unlikely thing. Imagine cooking ice cream!

The girls always requested Baked Alaska for their birthday cakes and often, when Michael was off on one of his business trips, Cassidy would make one for no reason other than the girls were as much in a party mood as she was. Usually they had it for dessert after a decidedly non-gourmet but much-loved dinner of wieners and beans, but even then the baked beans were homemade.

By the time Cassidy found out Michael had a mistress, the affair was nearly over anyway, so she didn't bother raising any dust about it. She might never have known except for the phone call at three in the morning. Not that she eavesdropped, but ever since the girls were babies it had been an unspoken way things got done that Cassidy was the one who got up during the night. After all, Michael needed his sleep because he worked so hard during the day whereas she could take a nap any time she wanted or needed one. So when the phone went off, Cassidy got up and answered it.

The woman on the other end of the line was weeping, and Cassidy wanted to say Now now, there there dear, everything will seem better in the morning, but it was nobody she knew, so it was none of her business, she just went back to bed and nudged Michael awake. "It's for you," she yawned, and crawled back into her still-warm spot. She probably would have gone to sleep in a minute if Michael had just talked in a normal voice, but he whispered. Not a little whisper which could only be heard by someone sitting next to him, but a stupid stage whisper, the kind a person has to use to be heard by the person on the other end of the phone. The whisper caught Cassidy's attention, enough that she sat up and listened long enough to know Michael was in a perfect fury. Just in case his fury had to be targeted on something, or someone, she lay back down, snuggled herself into a little half ball and yawned a few times, deliberately ignoring him. She didn't ask him anything about the phone call, he didn't offer anything. At no time did she demand to know whether or not he was having an affair, and at no time did he volunteer the information. But Cassidy knew there could be no other reason in the world for a weeping woman to phone an angry man in the middle of the night. She also knew her husband well enough to know that one phone call, on its own and by itself, would be enough to make him call a halt, even if things hadn't been in a rough patch to start with, and they must have been in a rough patch or why did the woman phone, and why did she weep?

The phone call, and the way they both dealt with it by not dealing with it, wasn't exactly a sharp corner in their relationship, but it certainly was the start of a slow curve, sending them in a different direction. Cassidy felt a huge relief. No matter how many stupid mistakes she might make, no matter how idiotic Michael might think she was, it was he, the perfect one, who had broken not only the moral and religious vows, but the legal civil contract they had made. Whatever Michael felt—and she was sure embarrassment was among his feelings, because Michael hated to feel anyone had outsmarted him, or even figured out what he was up to when he was being what he thought of as his private self—he seemed to consider Cassidy's silence another sign of her stupidity, or some kind of tacit permission to stray into any other bedroom he chose. He didn't flaunt his affairs, a person could be passed over for promotion if he got too sloppy or outrageous in his personal life, but Cassidy knew he made what she thought of as pit stops when he was away from home.

She didn't care. Whether they're vacuuming your floor, cleaning the drapes, washing the windows, doing the ironing or screwing your husband, if they're doing your job, they are your servant.

– II –

As soon as the police left, Cassidy cooked breakfast. It was several hours too early for breakfast, but by now she was wide awake and all the up-and-down the stairs had given her an appetite.

"Aren't you going to clean up this mess first?" Michael demanded.

"It's going to take days to clean it up. I don't want to wait that long for something to eat."

"Don't push it, Cassie. I'm tired and I'm pissed off and the last thing I need right now is lip from you."

"Would you like bacon and eggs?"

"No, I don't want bacon and eggs. A bowl of granola, some yogurt, maybe a slice of whole wheat toast." He sat at the table, his head in his hands, and for a moment Cassidy was filled with an emotion close to pity. He looked so harried, so unable to find a way out of this unexpected and inexplicable mess. "I've got a big meeting this morning," he said, his voice dull. "It's an important one, so of course there isn't a shred of clothing dry. I can take some stuff down to the 24-hour laundromat, but you can't put your suit through a dryer and this isn't the kind of meeting you can show up for in jeans and a tee shirt. Not to mention my shoes!"

"What time is the meeting?"

"Ten."

"Well, you know Bob Frazier, you golf with him some-times, and I'm sure if you give him a phone call and explain what happened, he'll open the store early for you."

He stared at her, then nodded. "I thought of that," he said. "It's just . . . damn it, I wasn't expecting to put out that kind of money right now."

"It's by way of being an investment," she said, putting his breakfast in front of him. "You've told me often enough to think of things in terms of investments or indulgences." She put her bacon in the pan. "You aren't indulging yourself with a new outfit, you're investing in this meeting and what it can mean." She had no idea where these words were coming from, they didn't sound like her at all.

Michael finished his breakfast and headed for the phone while Cassidy concentrated on getting her bacon just the right degree of crispy and frying her eggs exactly the way she liked them. When she had eaten, she went out to the garage and got the shop-vac and brought it into the house. She figured it didn't matter where she started, what she was up against was a house wet from basement to attic. It wasn't something could be cleaned up room by room because the water would continue to seep, drip, trickle, flow and ooze, while the basic chore facing her was to get as much of the water as possible out of the rugs and furniture and poured down the drain. She went down to the basement with a flash-light and flipped on the breaker box.

She went into the living room first. The sofa was sopping wet, the expensive stuffed chairs were sodden, she could hear the plink plink tink of drops falling from the drapes, from the ceiling, from the chairs, even from the piano nobody had played since the girls left home. She took the vacuum bag from the canister and started sucking up the water. In an amazingly short time the canister was full, so she took it to the bathroom and poured the water into the bathtub.

"Are you *nuts?*" Michael yelled. "God, I don't need a fried female on my hands, on top of everything else. Don't you know anything? The water will short out that thing and you'll wind up glowing in the dark."

"It's a wet-dry," she smiled. "If you're vacuuming up something dusty, you have to put in the bag or the dust will get into the motor and ruin it, but if it's just water or wet leaves or something, the hose goes in at the bottom of the canister and the suction motor is up in the lid area, so the liquid doesn't get to it."

"I can't believe we're standing here, wet to the skin, with plumbers due to arrive at any minute, having some kind of dopey conversation about vacuum cleaners." He shook his head, but at least he wasn't angry.

"Maybe after the vacuum cleaner conversation, we could have one about, oh, laundry detergent? They're always having laundry detergent dialogues on TV."

"Tub and tile cleaner," he agreed.

Somehow all the hot air about the shop-vac had diverted his attention from the fact Cassidy had switched on the breaker box. She hoped he'd be somewhere else when he realized it. China, maybe.

She went on hosing up water from the carpet and floor, taking the full canister to the bathroom and sending the dirty water down the drain. She couldn't think of a single other thing she could do. She had the doors open, but the sills were higher than the floors so the water didn't pour out. At best it pooled there, which made the job with the shop-vac easier, but not much easier.

She wished she could turn on the radio, but she knew Michael would have hell's own fit if she did. She'd already had to sidetrack him about the shop-vac, and that wouldn't last forever. Whatever else could be said about him, he wasn't a stupid man. Maybe a faery would fly through the open doorway and dance on the piano keys, providing some music. Although she probably wouldn't hear it over the noise of the vacuum.

There had been days in Cassidy's life when she had found herself turning on the vacuum and running the nozzle over floors and furniture which didn't really need cleaning, just because the noise blocked out all the other sounds, even blocked out her own thoughts and self-recriminations. Several times she'd spent the entire afternoon vacuuming simply to soothe herself, and she had gone into a kind of trance. The hours just disappeared, like cotton candy when you touch it with your tongue.

The plumbers arrived, Michael gave them their instructions, then he rushed off to get himself down to Bob Frazier's Men's Wear. Everyone considered it *the* place to get men's clothes, with the result that most of the working people in town went somewhere else. Bob's stock of jeans were expensive, and they weren't the same cut or style most of the workies preferred. Privately, Cassidy thought those jeans looked gorpy, a word she had learned from her daughters. But then nobody knew better than Michael, and Cassidy herself, just how low-rent and workie she really was. The class divisions in what we are told is a classless society are deep and wide, not easily bridged, and Cassidy had been born on the other side of the chasm.

Meanwhile, she just kept vacuuming water and pouring it down the bathtub drain. But then the plumbers wanted to know where the breaker box was and said they needed to turn off all electricity to the house, so that was that for the vacuuming. Cassidy sat on the plastic webbing chairs just outside the glass patio doors, wishing that when the girls had been taking piano lessons she'd had sense enough to sign on, too. But she hadn't, she'd been very busy. Even thinking back on it now she sometimes wondered how she'd managed to do all the things she'd done. The crude joke was, of course, that if she'd thought to ram the broom handle . . . and maybe she'd actually done that. Certainly whenever she thought back to that time she remembered it all to have been a total pain in the ass.

They'd both been good on the piano, never any foot-dragging about practice, never any sudden onset of sore throat or earache when it was time to go to lessons. They'd even seemed quite prepared to take classical lessons forever. But when they played for fun they played everything except classical. Even polkas.

Cassidy had such fun with her girls, such deep satisfactions. Sometimes she felt almost sorry for Michael because he'd missed so much, denied himself so much more. Michael didn't have much use for polkas, and Cassidy could still picture the look on his face when he realized not only did his daughters have fun playing polkas, they had even pooled their savings and bought a second-hand accordion so while one polka'ed on the upright, the other accompanied her on the squeezebox. Give him credit where it's due, though, all he said was, "I guess next we wind up learning the Hawaiian guitar."

It must feel very strange to have children and not be able to understand or accept or enjoy them, or feel free to let them make their own choices. Michelle's first real summer job was a shock to her father. He had expected her to smile widely as she rushed gladly into the several-hours-a-day job he had tentatively arranged for her with his firm. Instead, she very politely said no thank you, then left him staring in near horror when she told him she was going out on the *Shoes for the Baby* with Cassidy's brother Tim.

"A fish boat?" Michael made it sound like some kind of low-life bar.

"I'm the cook," Mikey laughed. "Fried egg sandwiches and canned pork and beans."

The very day school let out for the summer, Mikey was gone on the boat. She phoned every chance she got, but didn't come back until five days before school started up again. She came home tanned the colour of the piano, her hair sun-streaked, her eyes seeming to jump out of her face, with more money in her bank account than Cassidy could believe.

"I made more in the first week than I'd have made all summer at that office job," Mikey laughed. "And I didn't have to haul on the tasteful outfits and go sit inside breathing air everyone else had already breathed a dozen times or more."

That job was like a billboard, it marked the spot where Mikey and Michael started behaving toward each other in a completely different way. There were fewer arguments, which was a mercy because they'd had some terrible set-to's, and each went a gently diverging way until their paths were so far apart they'd have had to send faxes to each other if they wanted to talk. Michael neither understood nor approved of Mikey's choices, and she didn't care. The hard, sometimes brutally hard, work of fishing had put Mike in better shape than she'd ever been in, and she made the most of it. Suddenly she was up to her ears in sports, and if she wasn't coming home splattered with mud from a soccer game, she was streaming with sweat from basketball or bike racing.

And of course Corinne fell into some kind of hera worship. Anything big sis did was just fine. That drove the initial small wedge between her and her father, and Cassidy was the first to see it coming. She tried to talk to Michael about it but there wasn't much could be said. If two people don't understand each other, a third isn't going to interpret or to provide common ground. Funny how the differences drove Michael away from his daughters—the differences between the two girls were enormous but only brought them tighter together.

Mike wasn't interested in any schooling past grade twelve and would probably have quit before that except both Michael and Cassidy refused to hear a word about it. "I don't care if you never use it," Cassidy declared, feeling that she would start shouting if the debate lasted much longer, and that she might even lose it and slap Mike's face. "You aren't quitting school to be a fisher, young lady."

"I could do black cod and halibut and—"

"What you *will* do is socials and math!"

Mike didn't push it. But Cassidy knew she wasn't going to insist on college or university.

Corinne, on the other hand, sounded as if she wouldn't get out of school before her first old age pension cheque arrived.

"A plastic surgeon?" Michael looked like someone who didn't know whether to grin with pride or laugh with scorn.

"Reconstructive surgery," Corinne corrected him.

"Well, I can see being a doctor, and I can see specializing

is a good idea, it probably pays much better, but don't most women go into pediatrics or gynecology?"

"Not this woman. I considered neurology but it just didn't seem, I don't know, as interesting. I know I don't have the personality to go into research, so I'd be dependent on developments based on other people's work, and we know so little that a lot of stuff seems like shooting in the dark. Reconstructive, now, you get to *see* what needs done and then *see* how you did and if there's anything more you can do."

"With obstetrics you get even more to see," he suggested.

"Tell you what," Corinne grinned at him, and even dared to wink, "we'll *both* go to med school. You can take obstetrics, I'll take reconstructive, then we can open an office and every time you deliver an ugly kid, I'll fix it up for half price."

"Full price. We're not cutting any corners, kiddo, we're not bargain basement stuff."

It was amazing how Corinne could handle him. If Mikey had tried what Cori got away with, it would have kicked off a two-hour shouting match, and if Cassidy had tried it, she would have got a few whacks or even a good punch. Sometimes Corinne was downright cheeky, but Michael couldn't seem to get angry with her. He seemed to think she was a chip off the old block, another pea in the pod, exactly like him except for plumbing. Of the two, it was Mikey who was more like her father. But then Mikey had committed the all-time sin of not being a first-born son, and being the oldest, it was Mikey who had to scout the territory, then lead the way, training and educating her parents at every step. So Mikey was the one on whom the wrath was expressed.

Cassidy figured she was lucky Mikey didn't rebel earlier. She actually did finish grade twelve. Of course she didn't go to her graduation ceremonies and the big party afterwards. At the very time that was all starting to get under way, Mike was on the boat with Tim, catching fish and making money. Michael still held a grudge about that.

Cori graduated the correct way. Expensive formal gown, shoes, corsage, what Cassidy's family would call the whole nine yards. Photos, ceremony and Cori as valedictorian, while Michael watched, so proud Cassidy could have wept. There had been so many opportunities over the years for him to feel this full, and he'd missed them.

The plumbers quit searching at noon and took their metal lunch buckets to the kitchen where they could sit on dry wooden chairs. Cassidy offered to make them fresh tea or coffee but they said No thank you, gesturing at their thermoses. The electricity was still off at the breaker, but thank the goddess for gas ranges. She would have liked to sit with them, talk with them, but they seemed shy and uneasy when she was around so she went back out to the patio and stretched out on the lawn chair. The sun was warm on her face, she could hear the hummingbirds zizzing around the morning glory, heard bees busy in the lavender bed, and she realized she was hours short of sleep, and suddenly so tired she ached.

She was dimly aware of the sounds of Michael returning and she thought about making herself wake up to greet him. But then she heard him talking with the plumbers, and clearly heard them insisting they could find nothing wrong. It was odd how dozey she felt and yet how distinctly she could hear and even see them, but she couldn't be on her feet, standing in the doorway to the kitchen, because they were below her, as if she were up near the ceiling.

"What do you mean you can't find anything?" Michael

sounded dangerously angry, and Cassidy became very frightened. Michael angry was as bad as her father when he was drinking and preparing to make the world pay for his dissatisfactions.

"Maybe someone left a tap running."

"Why would I say there was no tap running if there was a tap running? Why would a person lie about that? And how could one tap flood the entire house?"

"Can't find any leaking pipes. 'Course, it's hard to tell with the walls as soaking wet inside as they are."

"One tap could make *all* the walls soaking wet inside?"

"Mister, if you want to pay by the hour for us to crawl around looking at perfectly good pipes, fine, I'm willing to do that for as long as you want."

"Listen, idiot, I had to go buy new clothes for work today because every other damn thing I owned was sodden. Not damp, drenched! One tap did that? Look at the place, damn it, it's the *top* of things got the worst of it."

"Well, yeah, a'course, if the tap was upstairs it'd leak through the floor, then drip through the ceiling."

"You're the damn drip here! We aren't talking a drip. We're talking a torrent, a deluge, we're talking most of the contents of this house ruined by water damage!"

Michael was so angry Cassidy backed away and went back to the patio and the relaxing lawn chair. Poor Michael, there was no way the plumbers were going to believe this hadn't been deliberately done, a tap or two or three left running on purpose so the insurance would pay for new rugs and furniture. Nothing he said would convince them, they hadn't seen it.

"There, damn it, I *told* you!" Michael yelped.

"Jeez aitch!" one of them breathed. Then, alarmed, "Where are you going?"

"Outside to take off my good clothes and leave them in the car! You think I want to put out another bundle of money for clothes for tomorrow? Go find the fucking tap, you water-on-the-brain numbskull. The two of you together are too stupid to shove shit through a funnel."

The plumbers might have walked out then and there, suggesting to Michael that he pound sand up his arse, but they had never seen rain falling inside a house before. They headed off to try to find the running tap. As they prowled through the place, getting more upset every minute, they talked about the possibility of worn threads on a tap, you turn it off but bit by bit it loosens and then begins to leak. They didn't find any such thing, but they talked about it as if it were right there in front of their eyes. Neither of them mentioned the fact the water was turned off at the intake connection as well as at the shut-off valve.

Their sandwiches were soaked and falling apart, the thermos coffee in their insulated metal caps was beaded with raindrops, and Cassidy still couldn't make herself waken.

The noise pulled her from her heavy sleep. She felt groggy and thick-headed, but there was enough noise to waken the dead. The plumbers were arguing with the City Inspector who was also arguing with the Plumbing Inspector and two men from the water department crew. The Fire Chief was demanding to know why the police had called him to the scene, several feral-looking people pointed TV cameras at anything which moved and a lot of stuff which didn't, and, attracted by the police cars and the fire truck and the backhoe that was busily digging up the lawn to get to the main water line, neighbours and others who weren't neighbours but were curious enough to qualify as such, were staring in from the lawn, peering in windows, even walking into the house by way of the back door and gaping at the rain showering down from the ceiling and sideways from the walls.

Michael was past being angry. He had stopped yelling at plumbers, stopped talking to police and city works inspectors. He leaned against a wet wall, his face grey, his hair rumpled. He'd pulled on a pair of wet jeans and a wet short-sleeved shirt and stuffed his soggy feet into wet sneakers, and he looked as if what he really wanted to do was run down the street screeching. When a TV reporter shoved a microphone in his face and the cameraperson aimed the lens and bright light in his face, Michael just shook his head. When the reporter persisted, Michael took the microphone in his hand, threw it to the floor and stomped on it.

"Your camera is next," he said quietly. "Get out of my house, get off my property, and learn some manners."

"This is my *job*," the reporter argued.

"Go do it somewhere else. If you were a mercenary they wouldn't let you do your job by shooting people or burning villages. This is an invasion of privacy and I have asked you to leave. If you don't go, I'm going to charge you with trespass."

Cassidy hoped he wouldn't do something awful, like punch out the two of them, but he seemed as numb as she felt. He went to the police and nattered at them until they eventually put the bum's rush on the TV crews. But no one could do anything about the curiosity seekers, so after a while Cassidy and Michael left their home and checked into a motel.

Michael had his dry clothes in his car, but Cassidy had to make a fast dash to get something to wear for dinner. Ordinarily she cleared all her purchases with Michael because he didn't think her taste in clothes was appropriate, but in all the fuss and rush she forgot and he didn't seem to care. She was feeling more than a bit blue, so she bought things in bright colours to cheer herself up a bit.

They went out for supper at the city's first Szechuan restaurant, which had opened a month earlier and was the trendiest place in town. Cassidy wondered why Michael had chosen it, everyone knew Szechuan was about the spiciest food a person could eat, and he didn't seem hungry. But she had a wonderful time trying out new foods, new tastes, new spices.

When they got back to the motel, he turned on the TV and sat glaring at it. Cassidy felt as if she was going to be sick. She knew the signs. Well, then, *why*, name of the goddess, *why* had he chosen to go to the Szechuan place? *Why* did things like that happen, anyway? He'd made the choice and hadn't liked the food and was probably still hungry but too shirty to admit it, and now he was going to sit working himself into a festering stew, and then the slightest little thing or even no thing at all would kick it off and he'd be out of control. Or maybe not out of control at all, maybe he'd been in a foul mood all along and the Szechuan place was just an excuse, or fuel, or his way of punishing himself before the fact.

And *why*, Cassidy wondered, did she spend so much time trying to rationalize the irrational, figure out the strange, and understand that which made no sense at all?

She had a bath in the little motel tub, which was so short she had to jackknife her legs. It wasn't relaxing at all, but maybe a person wasn't supposed to relax in a motel, just pay their money, watch some TV and sleep. Well then, since she didn't want to watch another Tough Guy movie or two hours of Victim TV, she'd go to bed and sleep. Small chance of getting into trouble, too, if you're fast asleep.

Unless someone is on the prod, and any excuse or no excuse at all will do. When they left the motel the next morning, anyone who saw Cassidy could tell that either she had been in a serious car accident or she had been beaten until Michael no longer felt like hitting her.

The police had strung yellow plastic streamers with black printing on them from tree to tree to bush to sapling all around the house. Police Line Do Not Cross. The TV people hadn't arrived yet, but the newspaper ones were there and the photographer got a few shots, so Cassidy's bruises and the cut to her left eyebrow were seen by probably three-quarters of the town. Cassidy wondered why several police were stationed around the house until she got inside and saw how much of her stuff had vanished. She didn't say anything, just looked at the heavy-set older cop, who shrugged almost apologetically.

"Vandals," he sighed. "Someone called in about ten-thirty or eleven last night and said folks were walking off with your stuff, so . . . " He shrugged again.

"Heavens," she said mildly, "wouldn't you wonder what a body wanted with a sodden upholstered chair? By the time they get it dry it will have gone mouldy inside, and every time anyone sits on it, this musty smell will rise up, anyone with allergies will get sick and—"

"Oh shut up, Cassidy, you're babbling," Michael snapped.

The cop looked at him, then looked at Cassidy's face, then looked at Michael again. Michael turned away, his eyes half shut.

"Did you get someone to check over those bruises and cuts on your face?" the cop asked.

"No." She smiled at him, lopsidedly because of the swelling in her bottom lip. "It's not as bad as it looks, I've had worse."

Michael stiffened, and the crimson climbing up the back of his neck was like a promise she would get worse again, and soon.

"You know it's assault and that's against the law?"

"Yes." She felt so calm she wondered if he'd punched something loose inside her head, rattled or addled or fractured something. "The thing is, you see, you can't keep them there forever and when they get out they're even nastier."

Until now, she had always tried to cover up the truth. There must be any number of people who thought her one of the most clumsy, accident-prone fools in the world, if they believed what she had said to explain the marks. When she tried to pass off her broken arm as a skiing accident, and Sally Martel had blurted "I didn't even know you skied!" Cassidy had raised her heavily casted arm and said, "Obviously, I don't, at least not well," and Sally had gladly believed her. Why not? If she didn't believe it, she might have felt she ought to do something, and what could anybody do?

Maybe the only one who could do anything was Michael himself, and she couldn't trust him. He'd already done enough—done too much, in fact.

What hadn't been lifted by vandals was starting to suffer. Cassidy found the phone books, swollen and almost useless. She managed to locate a yellow pages listing for a moving and storage company and asked them to come and get the piano. She couldn't think of anything else she wanted to put in storage, but Michael told her she was an idiot and phoned the company back to ask if they could also take the china cabinet, the TV, the stereo and more. Cassidy lost interest before he finished listing everything he wanted stored, and went to her bedroom.

She looked at her reflection in the mirror and shook her

head. The brightly coloured clothes were fine as long as you didn't look at what they were hanging from. In fact they had looked better on the hanger in the store. She almost laughed, Michael said her laughter was often inappropriate. The bright colours clashed with the duller hues of the bruises and lumps. She wondered if she should go back down and try to find something which would colour co-ordinate with her swollen eye.

The rain still drizzled from the ceilings and walls, and now she was sure it was oozing up from the flooring as well. Someone had closed an upstairs door and when she opened it, water gushed out as if from a broken water main. Maybe if they shut all the doors and windows, water would eventually spurt out of the chimney and the entire house would fill up until the walls bulged and the whole thing burst open, flooding the yard, eroding the flower beds, dumping silt and uprooted rhododendrons all over the road.

On the shelf above the rod in her clothes closet, she found the big purple backpack Mikey had given her for her birthday. "So you can come out on the boat with me," she had said softly, and both of them knew how much was unsaid between them. Into the pack Cassidy stuffed wet clothes from her drawers and from her closet. She didn't have to worry about starched white shirts or neatly pressed suits, she could take her things to the laundromat and dry them there.

She took Mikey's keys from her underwear drawer and put them in the little front pocket on the purple backpack. Michael would want the car again, and Cassidy didn't feel like walking to the laundromat or taking a municipal bus either. Not with a face in the shape hers was in. But she wanted dry clothes, and there was only one way she could think of to get them.

Michael sloshed into the bedroom with a list of things he wanted her to do. Pack this, phone these, arrange for something else. She didn't tell him to shove his list up his nostril, she just looked at him as if he were a form of life she hadn't previously encountered, then lifted her pack and walked past him. She'd never done anything like that before, but then she hadn't had a couple of burly cops downstairs before, either.

They understood immediately. Not one word needed spoken, they just walked with her to the garage and waited while she got Mikey's Tracker started and backed it out, then turned it, not even caring that the wheels left the paved driveway and dug tracks into the obsessively manicured lawn.

"Thank you very much," she smiled.

"Any time, ma'am," the paunchy cop said politely. He handed her his business card and she put it in her purse, then drove away from the house and told herself she was only going to the Pink Elephant laundromat.

As she drove past Michael's car she noticed its windows were heavily fogged, and she realized with some form of glee that it was raining in the Buick, as well. She laughed, and the sound of her laughter made her think of faery bells—long unused and a bit stiff at the clapper, but still functional.

– III –

Wile her clothes whirled in the dryer, Cassidy went to the bank. She opened the safety deposit box and took everything out of it. House papers, insurance papers, Canada savings bonds, RRSP certificates, stocks, bonds, anything up to and including the girls' birth certificates and the marriage licence. She put everything except the marriage licence and marriage certificate in her purse. Those she ripped into four more or less equal parts and left them in the box for the next inquiring soul.

Then she went upstairs, presented the term deposit certificates, RRSPs and Canada savings bonds, and found herself unnecessarily going on to the teller about the broken pipe or whatever it was which had just about ruined everything in the house. "And," she said chattily, "they still don't have a clue where it's coming from so obviously we're going to have to make other arrangements. We can get a condo lease for three months, but, of course, it's empty. And we'll need new stuff anyway when we move back into the house ..." On and on she chatted, as if she had all day to visit, as if everything was hunky-dory, as if she didn't have a face like a disaster zone. "It's awful," she confided, and touched her lip ruefully. "Something like that happens in the middle of the night and of course the damn lights don't work because of all the water, and you're so upset and scared you forget where the stairs are from second to first floor, even though you've been using them three or four or five times a day for the past twenty-some years!" She made herself laugh. "As if there wasn't already enough to contend with, there I am going over and over in the dark and Michael yelling *what's going on?*"

"Sounds like a horror show," the teller agreed, smiling and listening, counting out hundred dollar bills.

The first thing she did upon leaving the bank was to duck into Saan's and get herself a pair of GWG jeans, not the least bit what Michael would have approved of, not the least bit tailored-looking and gorpy. She also got new white athletic socks, thick cotton, not the pretty thin kind Michael found appropriate, and a pair of real sneakers, Nike high-tops, not the little pink-trimmed ones she'd felt she had to wear for so many years.

She changed in the toilet cubicle at the laundromat, then folded her dry clothes, put them in her purple pack and went back to Mikey's car. She knew, deep in her heart, where it counted, that the rain in the house had become a torrential downpour; knew, too, without having the slightest idea how she knew, the rain was falling steadily in Michael's car and in his office as well. It almost seemed to her as if entire portions of the world were weeping. Then again, tears were salty, and what had been falling wasn't. It must be another one of her dumb ideas, the kind almost guaranteed to get you a slap in the face. Still, if tears could be unsalted, that's what a person could be forgiven for thinking were falling almost nonstop on and over and into the souvenirs of the last thirty-plus years of Cassidy's life.

The lawyer she went to see was young and blond and had a picture of his family on his desk, not a posed studio portrait but an enlarged snapshot of a young woman in shorts and a tee shirt having a water fight with two pre-schoolers on the front lawn. The house in the background was at least as old as the lawyer, and it hadn't cost a fraction of what Michael had paid for his sailboat two years before, or the huge sums he had poured into it ever since. The name on the door told anyone interested that the lawyer's name was Alan Bailey, but Cassidy had no idea what all the initials after the name meant. Right now Alan Bailey was looking at the papers she had placed on his desk. When he looked up at her, she saw the half smile of approval.

"This," she said, putting the cash on the table as his eyes widened, "is what I want. He can have the rest. It's more than fair." The lawyer was grinning now. "He gets the house, wet as it is. The last tax assessment said it was worth two hundred and fifty-five thousand, but I imagine it will have devaluated since it started to rain inside. However," she pushed forward the insurance papers, "I'm sure he's covered for everything under the sun and I'm sure there's no way the company can call *this* an act of God. When God's in charge, it rains outside. He has a thirty-two-thousand-dollar Buick, he's got fifty thousand dollars worth of boat, trailer and motor, plus his sailboat, and I have no idea what it's worth, I just know people whistle when they see it. With that sailboat he has a Zodiac for a lifeboat, and I don't know what that's worth either, but I bet they aren't standing on the street giving them away. And these," she pushed some more papers at him, "the bank said they couldn't cash without both of us being there and signing in the presence of a bank officer. I told them we'd both be in tomorrow or the day after, but I won't be here. And probably he won't be able to cash them without my signature. And you can tell his lawyer that I won't sign them unless Michael agrees to this division of assets. He'll argue, bluster, holler and fight tooth and nail, but as far as I'm concerned this is not negotiable. I get this money, he gets the rest, and if he will insist on being a prick, I won't sign these papers and he won't get *this* money either."

"You've really thought this out." Alan Bailey's voice was calm, but there was no hint he was trying to butter her up or soothe her.

"I haven't really," she confessed. "I don't have any experience with this kind of thing. But it's as if—oh, I don't know, as if a person listens to other people's horror stories and whether she knows it or not, she learns something. Although I have to tell you," and she smiled her lopsided smile again, "it took me about three times as long to learn it as it ought to have done."

"Have you been to a doctor?"

"I'm going there when I'm finished here. I wanted to get the jump on him. Besides which, I have a sneaking suspicion if I'd gone to Emergency first, it would have been a couple of days before I could do the rest of what I've already done, and that means Michael would have got to the bank and the safety deposit box before I did." She took a tissue from the box on his desk and dabbed at her nose. What was leaking wasn't so much blood any longer as it was some kind of blood-tinged, yellow-streaked clear fluid.

"Do you have any idea who will be representing your husband? Soon to be ex-husband."

"Probably the same lawyer he's had since the year dot."

She gave Alan the name of the lawyer and he nodded. "If you really need some ammunition, you might let my soon-to-be-ex know that I'm quite prepared to phone his lawyer and tell him about the ongoing affair Michael has been having with his lawyer's wife."

The lawyer laughed out loud. "You *do* have things organized," he said. "You want me to drive you to Emergency? You look really awful."

"I don't feel really awful. I'll be fine."

She'd been right. If she'd gone to the Emergency Ward first, she'd never have made it to Saan's, the Pink Elephant, the bank or the lawyer's office. They took a few x-rays, asked her if she'd had breakfast, seemed very relieved when she said not yet, and the next thing she knew she was in a hospital bed, they were putting an IV in the back of her left hand, and she had just enough presence of mind to give them Cori's phone number before whatever was in the IV started making her fuzzy and dry-mouthed. When she swam up out of the grey cotton fog she knew she'd completely missed breakfast, lunch and supper, and would miss any chance of a cup of tea if she didn't wake up soon.

Cori was sitting in an ugly plastic-covered turquoise chair, calmly reading a book at least twice as big as *War and Peace*.

"Cor?" Cassidy managed. "I feel like I'm going to sneeze."

"You won't," Cori assured her, "but it will feel like that for a few days, maybe a week or more." She got out of the chair, put the huge book where her butt had been, moved to the bedside and kissed Cassidy on the cheek. "Before you ask, heart, I'll tell you. When the packing comes out and the bandages come off you're going to have a whole new nose. The one you came in here with was absolutely smashed. But not to worry, I supervised the job myself, so you know you're gonna be gorgeous, right? I'm quite sure your eyebrow is going to heal so well there won't even be a noticeable scar. Your lip will take a while to heal and you might have some numbness there and probably some scarring and thickening that we'll have to fix later on, but it won't be a big deal." Cori looked away, and Cassidy realized that beneath the professional exterior her younger daughter was fighting anger and sorrow. "The best person we've got, besides me, fixed the cracks in your head. I saw the x-rays and I have to tell you it's one of the wonders of all time that you were even conscious, let alone moving around, driving Trackers and buying new jeans."

"How . . . ?"

"You yap when you're coming out of anaesthetic. Oh, and your lawyer knows you're here, knows what all has been done to fix you up, and he and I took several rolls of colour film, for evidence. I found some cop's business card in your purse and phoned him, so he's been here with a video camera, also for evidence, and at this point it's all out of your hands. You don't have to press charges or anything, the police have the family asshole sitting in a cell."

"Well, at least it's warm and dry in there." Cassidy struggled to sit up, then wished she hadn't, because gongs were sounding in her head. "I felt better before you guys got busy fixing me up," she tried to joke. "And I'd commit unmentionable obscenities for a cup of tea."

She got it. She also got a bowl of chicken soup. "I'd rather have hot and sour from the Szechuan place," she muttered, but she ate the canned chicken noodle.

"I'll get you hot and sour for lunch," Cori promised.

"I have to pee."

"No, you don't, it just feels that way. You've got a catheter."

"My mouth tastes like a camel died in there."

"We can fix that. Your toothbrush and stuff was in your pack, so I put it in your bedside table, and got you some mouthwash too, the kind that doesn't sting like fury, because the inside of your mouth is a mess. You might have a couple of teeth that feel as if they're a bit loose but—"

"Yeah, let me guess, they aren't, the way I don't have to pee and don't have to sneeze, right?"

"You got 'er, heart. We'll get you cleaned up and comfortable, then we'll order a nice big needle rammed into your butt and you'll sleep until morning."

"I'm sure glad I was the mom and you were the kid. It would have been hell the other way around."

"It was pretty much hell a lot of the time the way it was," Cori corrected. "It just about drove Mikey and me to screaming fits the way he treated you. And worse was the way you behaved as if he not only had the right to do it, it was almost your fault. But we won't talk about that now, okay?"

"No. We might never talk about it, okay?"

"No, not okay at all. Mikey says to tell you she'll fly down over her three-day closure and see you then. She also says if you need any money—"

"I have money," Cassidy remembered then, and tried to sit up, startled and suddenly very afraid. "My purse! What happened to—"

"It's okay, Momma." Cori sounded so much like Cassidy's Aunt Joan that, in the flash of a moment, things got confused and the inside of Cassidy's head felt stuffed, just too full of too much. "I have your purse," Cori went on. "And I found your money when I found that cop's card. Do you want me to put it in the bank for you? The money, not the card."

"No. After all, I took it *out* of the bank," and she let Cori ease her back down onto the pillow. It felt good to just let the weakness take over, pretend she was a child again, pretend it was Aunt Joan who was fussing her, hand over everything she'd been trying so hard to get for all those puzzling, frightening years. "He'd find a way to get it out, too," she yawned.

Cori was grinning and saying something, but Cassidy just couldn't pull herself together long enough to hear or respond. Her face was sore, her entire body ached, and she couldn't quite understand why, now that they all said they had fixed her up, she hurt worse than she'd hurt when she left the sodden house.

The next time she wakened, two nurses and a doctor who looked too young to have started med school, let alone finished it, stood at the bedside, checking her and her chart. The doctor seemed puzzled. Maybe even more than puzzled. The nurses looked as if it was taking every drop of patience and courtesy they possessed not to just walk away and leave Beaver Cleaver to imitate Doctor Kildare all by himself.

"Are you sure?" he persisted.

"Doctor, this patient came here from the recovery room, was put in this bed, the sides of the bed were raised, and, except for a brief period of time when she wakened and spoke to her daughter, she's been asleep. She did not roll out of bed, climb out of bed, fall out of bed or—"

"But there's no mention of these!" He realized Cassidy was awake and handed the chart to the very indignant nurse.

"Can you hear me?" he asked.

"Of course I can hear you, son, you're standing so close to my bed you're nearly in it with me." But she smiled. And immediately regretted doing it because it made her face ache.

The boy-doctor asked her some questions, she answered

them. He looked at her fingers and at the beds of her nails, he pressed the back of her hand, he checked her arms and legs and softly said things to the indignant nurse who was making notes on a pad of paper. The other one, the not-quite-so-indignant one, was drawing a picture, quite a crude one, and marking on it. It was a drawing of a reclining woman, about three steps up the evolutionary ladder from a stick figure. Odd that the hospital would tolerate a thing like that. You'd think they'd discourage doodling.

Cassidy didn't much feel like being part of the scene any more. It was like an amateur theatre farce, any minute now the Romantic Stranger would come through the door. He would be the catalyst and his effect on these three would change forever the way they related to each other. Some sort of huge international, universal, cosmic truth would be revealed to the audience. Like a change is as good as a rest, or one swallow does not a summer make, and then the curtain would fall and the audience, once again instructed and shown the path to enlightenment, would clap dutifully and go home.

Some part of her brain heard them trying to get her to waken and answer their questions, but it wasn't a part she had to pay attention to and she very much wanted to ignore them. She knew she wouldn't be able to give them any answers and having to say *I don't know* so many times would only make her feel depressed. So she ignored them and after a time they went away. When they returned they brought some others with them, and she knew from the sudden flashes of light which disturbed her even though her eyes were closed, that someone was taking pictures. She also knew that it was an absolute invasion of privacy. Maybe she'd talk to her new lawyer about it.

Mikey was the one brought her back up from her comfortable hidey-hole, and she wakened alert and smiling.

"Mom, you're scaring the spit out of everyone," Mikey said firmly. "You have to find some way to stay awake for a while."

"I'm awake," Cassidy sighed.

"Well, don't make it sound like the end of the world. Cori filled me in so you don't have to."

Mikey was tanned, deeply tanned, but Cassidy didn't bother giving her the lecture about the ozone layer, the holes, the radiation, the skin cancer and the death. She knew what Mikey would say in reply.

"You look a bit tired," she said instead.

"Nothing a few hours' sleep won't cure. You look like you've been run over by a double-decker tour bus. They're very worried about that, you know. They thought someone might be coming in here and beating on you with a stick— you look about ten times worse than you did when they brought you back from the operating room. Have you got any idea what happened?"

"Me? Mikey, I'd laugh but it would hurt."

"Well, I didn't see you when you came in here so I don't know what you looked like than, but right now you look as if every whack he ever gave you has decided to show itself. For a while they were taking pictures every half hour, so they could document the increase in the number of bruises and welts."

"Can that happen? Can a bruise show itself six or ten or however many years later?"

"I never heard of it but then there's lots of stuff I've never heard of so what does that mean?" Mikey actually grinned. "The big kerfuffle right now is which pictures will be entered as evidence in court. His lawyer, who shall remain nameless because I don't want anyone to think I know the sucker, is arguing like hell to have the later ones blocked and your lawyer already has his own copies and says he intends to present them in court. The old man is out now, incidentally, and he's as mad as a wet hen but your lawyer is about six jumps ahead of him and you don't have to worry, he won't show up here to harangue you. If he shows his nose he's back in jail. He wanted to charge you with theft because of the money you cleared out of the bank accounts." Mikey chuckled again. "How did you manage that, anyway?"

"Oh, I just forged his name, is all. I've seen his signature so many times over the years that it's probably more familiar than my own, so I took the papers out to the parking lot, signed his name in all the appropriate places, then went back in and signed my own in front of the teller. I'd have signed more if it hadn't been that some of them were the kind where the body has to be visible, and seen while signing. If I could I'd have taken it all, but . . . oh well, it's better than nothing which is probably what I'd have wound up with if I'd done it any other way. How's the fishing?" Cassidy wanted the subject changed. It was boring her so badly she considered going back to sleep.

"Good. Prices are the shits, of course. Amazing how sockeye is worth bugger-all and there's an oversupply of it right up until the damn season is over, and then all of a sudden wham-o, the companies realize nine-tenths of the world is near starving, the price goes up like a hot air balloon, and they whine about a shortage of fish. Philistines. Each and every one of them. Philistines."

"You know how it is. They heard God say 'Go ye forth, multiply and fill the earth,' and they're doing it."

"Cori ought to be here soon." Mikey's face lit up when

she mentioned her sister's name, her eyes sparkled and she smiled broadly. "While she's visiting, I'll head off to get you anything your little heart desires for supper. That yellow stuff dripping into your veins can't be much by way of a meal."

"I think supper might have to be something I don't have to chew very much," Cassidy said, explored the inside of her mouth with her tongue.

"Yeah, that's got them worried, too. You're probably going to get written up in every medical journal in the world. The woman whose teeth fell out while she was in a coma."

"Oh, they're not *out*," Cassidy protested. "I can feel them with my tongue, they're just very . . . shortish."

"Shortish? Sounds like a dance. First we'll dance the polecat, then we'll do the shortish." Mikey leaned forward. "Let's see."

Cassidy dutifully opened her mouth but her attention was rivetted on Mike's face, on how fast her expression was changing, how rapidly her eyes blinked.

"Jeez, Mom, you're . . . you're growing new ones!"

"Is that what it is? Well listen, let me tell you, I really know now why babies cry so much when they're teething. Mind you, it does feel as if it's happening in my whole body! Teething, toeing, fingering . . . and facing."

"They must have you on some real good drugs." Mike pretended to be amused, but there was something in her eyes, something new.

"How are the kids? Have you seen them yet?"

"I only got here a while ago. They're not back yet from summer program so I'll see them later. And I don't remember anything like 'summer program' when I was a kid. You think all this scheduled stuff is good for them? I mean it's like they get born and they get slid into this regulated time-motion management thing they probably aren't going to get out of for the rest of their life."

When Michael had found out Mikey was pregnant, he had just about gone into orbit. When he found out she had no intention of getting married and even less intention of sharing with anyone the name of the father, he nearly exploded. But what really sent him into repeated bouts of fury was that Mikey didn't care. He finally reached the point where he was snarling at Cassidy that if Mikey didn't smarten up and stop being such a pill he was going to lay down the law and tell her not to bother darkening his door again. Mikey, on the phone, said she didn't much feel like coming around for a visit when "the old fart" was home, but she *did* want to see her mother, so why didn't they meet at Mikey's place instead of her parents' house. When Michael finally clued in that Cassidy had been seeing Mikey often but he hadn't, he walloped her, but only in places where the bruises didn't show. He did that a lot. Sometimes he took off his belt, as if she was little again, trying to cope with her dad, and he whaled away on her. But unlike her dad, he didn't leave marks where anyone else would see them. After all, he had his position in the community to consider.

When Liberty was born and Cassidy went to stay a few days with Mikey to make sure she knew how to hold, bath, change, handle and breastfeed properly, Michael was, thank God for small mercies, out of town for a week and a half. He returned from his trip and found Cassidy back home again, but he knew she'd been gone because each time he phoned he'd got the answering tape.

"Where have you been?" he demanded, and she knew no matter what she said, she was in for it big time.

"Helping Mikey look after Liberty." She could hear the cringing in her voice and hated herself for it.

"Liberty? What in hell kind of name is that for a baby?" Then his face changed and he blurted out, "My God, it's not *black*, is it?"

"She, not it, she. And she has reddy-blond hair, white skin and no telling what her eye colour is going to be, right now it's that funny baby-colour." She tried to make her voice pleasant, and she prayed overtime that he would get so focussed on the child's name that he would forget he was trying to pick a fight.

But some things Michael wouldn't forget. From some things he could hardly ever be sidetracked. "I must have phoned half a dozen times!" he growled, cold as the inside of a walk-in freezer. Any answer Cassidy gave would be the wrong one. "I damn near phoned the police to ask them to check and make sure you weren't lying dead on the floor with your throat slit." He was walking stiffly, almost marching, heading upstairs with his briefcase in one hand and his suitcase in the other. She didn't follow him. If she did he might lose it and slam her with the briefcase, something he'd done two or three times in the past.

Nothing she did or didn't do, nothing she said or didn't say made any difference. Within two and a half hours she was throbbing from head to toe, and not with passion.

He was not off on a trip when Freedom arrived. Even so, Cassidy went over, prepared to stay and help, but Mikey hugged her tightly, wept a bit, then said no, she knew full well what had happened last time. "I'm getting a homemaker for a few days," she said, as firmly as she could with her face damp with tears. "You come over when he's at work, tell him you went shopping or something. Buy him some of those goddamn maroon ties he wears all the time. Some of those black socks. Maybe even go hog wild, Mom, and buy him yet another plain white shirt! Prove you've been shopping. For him. That's what his BS is all about, anyway. One way or the other he will dominate your attention."

But Cassidy wasn't sure Mikey's analysis was anywhere near right, and who would know better, anyway? A small part of it was because Michael had no control over Mikey's life, so he compensated by controlling a larger and larger part of Cassidy's. But mostly, she figured, he beat on her because he could. Exactly the way her father had beat on her, and worse. Because he could. And Cassidy had no sooner managed to finish school, get a job and find a very small apartment of her own, than she met Michael, and immediately felt she'd known him all her short life. She had no way of knowing how close to the truth she was. Trained by one christless tyrant, she up and married another. And for years told herself it wasn't true she'd hopped from frying pan to fire. After all, she argued with herself, Michael did not beat his children, or abuse them in other, worse ways.

Except the harm it does a child to see her mother beaten to a bruised and bleeding pulp, over and over again.

Cassidy did not ask who the father or fathers of the girls was. If Mikey thought it was in any way important, she would tell her. Whoever he or they were, they did not figure large in Mikey's plans for the rest of her life.

"Probably your rotten brother Tim!" Michael sneered. "It's about on a par with the rest of his life." Cassidy did not answer, she knew Michael was on the prod, looking for a way to kick himself into his crazed mode. "Makes more money running dope than he ever makes out there catching fish."

She looked up at him in surprise. "I beg your pardon?" she gulped.

"You heard me. He's been pulled over twice, hasn't he? Log book check, he said. Log book check my backside, they were looking for dope. It's obvious. You can't tell me that idiot and his crew of misbegotten fools can go out there and catch fish when nobody else can!"

Cassidy didn't dare answer. Not just because she didn't want to fetch herself a good swat, but because she wasn't at all sure Michael wasn't correct. Tim was her favourite sib, but that didn't mean he wasn't raised in the same next-best-thing-to-hillbilly environment, with uncles who ran their own still and sold moonshine and a father who was more than ready to do anything at all. And Mikey, well, Cassidy might *hope* not, but what did she really know? What did anyone on shore really know about those who were out there bobbing on the frigid waves?

And Mikey was making good money, no denying that. The part-time homemaker became a full-time nanny, a woman from El Salvador who bore the visible scars of torture, a woman who had been incarcerated for years, then let out briefly, and only the paranoia of prison had saved her. She heard a car door slam in the middle of the night, she heard male voices, and she was wide awake, grabbing her shoes and heading out of her room, down the stairs in the apartment building, down from her room to the basement. At about the time several large men were coming through the front door of the building, one small woman was going out a window in the basement. The window was almost impossible to see from the outside, hidden as it was by flowering shrubs. She crawled behind the shrubbery and pressed against the side of the building, past the ones left to guard the outside.

Maria figured it all for a miracle, because just when she got to the back of the building, God sent clouds to hide the moon. The darkness was almost complete. And a dog fight broke out on the street in front of the house. The noise sent the guards running. Maria ran, too. She sneaked through the little access gate in the tall fence around the back yard, then headed down the alley, her shoes still held tightly in her fear-clammy hand. She was blocks away before she dared duck into a dark doorway and slip her shoes onto her feet.

Prison had taught her to sleep in her clothes. Other prisoners had taught her to never put her money in the bank but to wear it in a money belt around her waist. She didn't have much, but at least she had it.

When asked how she had managed to escape she said only, "I walked. I found a refugee camp. Finally, I came here."

Cassidy knew Maria had a story to tell, and knew too the chances of her telling it publicly were slim. Too many of her family had been rounded up and shot in retribution for her escape. A story told publicly, or worse, written and published, could mean certain death for the survivors as well.

One thing was certain. Maria loved the kids. Another certain thing was the kids loved Maria. They grew up speaking both Spanish and English, and if Michael had known that would have angered him too. But he never asked about them, and Cassidy didn't offer any information. She didn't even dare hang up pictures of them where anyone might see them.

Well, as soon as she got out of this place, she'd remedy that!

"Cori tells me you said you didn't need any money. And," Mikey grinned widely, "she told me why you didn't. But if ever you do, please let me know. Let me do that much at least."

"I promise, dear. If I need money, I'll let you know," and she laughed. "Your father always insisted you and Tim weren't out there catching fish as much as you were out there running dope."

"You want to know about dope? Everything there is to know about dope? Just say his name. If ever there was dope, it's him." They both laughed. But Cassidy filed away for future pondering the fact Mikey had in no way denied the charge. Was she? She certainly seemed to have a lot of money. Big old house, renovated and what they laughingly called "gentrified," sitting on five acres of land, all of it paid for in full. Was it salmon which had provided the money or something else? After all, everyone said there were hardly any salmon left to catch.

Cori arrived and spent a boringly long time checking Cassidy, doing the doctor thing, concentrating particularly on her face. Finally Cassidy put up her hand, took Cori by the forearm and shook her head gently. "Please, baby." She felt as if she was about to weep. "No more of this. Please."

"Momma, there are doctors lined up from here to the airport hoping for a chance to see you. Grown men and women who would give anything to be allowed to study your chart."

"Let them. Run off copies on the photocopier if you want. But I don't want to be poked, probed or peered at any more. I'm going to be okay, truly I am. I feel much better already."

"Momma, listen. The policeman said that when he saw you, you had black eyes and a slightly swollen face. The bank people said you had black eyes, a swollen face and some bruises on your arm. The lawyer said you had all that plus an ear that looked like the stereotypical cauliflower. The first examination here showed all that plus some bruising on your legs. Then, for the next several days, every time someone looked at you, you were worse, up to and including lacerations. They want that explained. Want it explained so badly they've had video cameras trained on you for days! And I've seen the film. You aren't hitting yourself, you aren't slamming your face into the wall, all you're doing is lying there, in what might just as well be called a coma. And then there's the small matter of your teeth. Teeth don't fall out in one afternoon and then start to grow again before the next day. It just doesn't happen. The tooth faery doesn't visit anyone over the age of eight! But she must have practically moved in here with you. *That* is why you get peered at, prodded, poked and studied."

"I know all that. But it isn't as if it was something I chose to have. And I'm getting better. My face feels almost normal now."

"It is almost normal, Momma. But this morning it wasn't, okay?"

"Please don't be stern with me. I'm very tired. Not sleepy! Just very very tired."

Mikey ducked out while Cori was doing her doctor thing, and, true to her word, came back after a while with food. Wonderful food. "Not from a restaurant or cafe, either," she crowed. "From Maria. She says there's more. She's bringing the kids up, they'll be here soon."

Cassidy kept herself awake for the visit. She packed away so much of Maria's food she thought she might very well look as if, along with every other physical oddity and medical puzzle she seemed to have developed, she had grown a pumpkin in her belly. Unless her skin split along the spine because it could no longer contain all that food in her.

The girls were very quiet and had obviously been briefed ahead of time, probably by Maria, possibly by Mikey as well.

They held Cassidy's hand, they cuddled, they tried hard not to stare at her, and they were obviously upset.

"My darlings," Cassidy said gently, "I don't want you to feel so badly about this. I'm getting better. I'll be out of here very soon. And then you can help me look for a place to live."

"You can live with us!" Liberty sounded just like Mikey, ready to take charge of anything that seemed to need it. "We've got lots of room."

"But I want a place of my own."

"You can have your own room. You could have two of them, side by side, upstairs."

"Not rooms, dear. Almost all my life I've lived in houses other people considered to be theirs. Now I want a place of my own. Maybe not a *house* house, but you can buy apartments and condos and townhouses and such-like and have someone else take care of things like mowing the lawn and cleaning the gutters. And you can help me look for just exactly the perfect one!"

She was ready to leave at least a week before they were ready to let her go. She could have insisted, demanded, persisted and forced them to release her, but instead she tried hard to co-operate. Her every weight gain was charted, her urine analyses alone would have made a three-inch stack of paper, she donated to the vampires in the lab every morning and every evening and had more pictures taken than most movie stars. They even had a dentist come in to examine her new teeth.

"Could I take an x-ray?" the dentist asked. Well, at least he asked! More than could be said for most.

"I'm going to glow in the dark at this rate," she smiled, and the dentist headed off eagerly to make the arrangements. And when all the fuss and taradiddle was finished the dentist

studied his films, stared at her, and said, "I have no explanation for this at all. I'm looking at a full set of brand new,
absolutely healthy adult teeth, each one of them beautifully
aligned with the others, a perfect bite and, I might add, a
gorgeous smile. I've never even heard of this happening
before, let alone seen it myself. Would you mind if I wrote an
article about this and submitted it?"

"As long as it doesn't require any input from me you can
do just about anything you want. And if any of them start to
rot, get loose, fall out, or hurt I promise you'll be the one I go
to see." Cassidy hated going to the dentist at the best of times,
but she felt safe making this promise because she didn't think
her new teeth were going to bother her in any way.

And finally they let her go. The girls were disappointed
when she didn't move in with them and Maria. But Cassidy
was afraid that if she did, she'd settle in like a flea in a carpet
and she didn't want to do that. So she moved in with Cori for
a while. "Just in case I need my own personal physician," she
teased. But she did remember her promise to Liberty and
Freedom, and took them with her when she started looking
for her own place.

– IV –

Cassidy looked at apartments, she looked at town-houses, she looked at duplexes and triplexes and she looked at condos. She looked at places she thought ought to be called at least one of those names and found they weren't that at all, they were called by yet other titles. She got so sick of seeing empty places painted all white, or other empty places painted in combinations of grey and pink or teal and raspberry that she almost gave up on ice cream, especially the kinds which came in any of those colours.

The girls gave up searching with her. For them it was a one-week wonder, and theirs was a five-day week. They both began their campaign to get her to stay with them, forever'n'ever 'cause we love you so much. Cori even dropped some hints about the apartment in her building, just down the hallway, Mom, and no problem about price, either.

Cassidy was not the least bit interested in the ultra-modern standoffish design of Cori's apartment but didn't know how to say so without sounding ungrateful. She was afraid years and years of going along with someone else's idea of what was good and right and appropriate and proper would propel her into doing something silly, like signing the purchase papers. She began to feel a knot in her stomach, began to resent the day after day of looking at places which were so much like places she had already seen she often felt she'd been there before.

And then, sheer and total luck took a hand. Cassidy was supposed to meet the real estate agent at ten in the morning in front of a newly constructed strata title development. She knew before she left Cori's apartment and got in her car what she'd see when she got where she was supposed to be going. Raw dirt. Probably acres of raw dirt with the crossbar tracks of heavy equipment crisscrossing it. The building would be all sharp corners and extreme angles, the balconies designed like fins so people could put large or tall plants in the narrow end and block the view of other people on either side. The windows would be large and the promise would be that once the landscaping was in, there would be a view of the flower beds. And she knew she would look through it pretending to be very interested and then she would say she was going to think about it, and go home and try to forget it completely.

But on the way to the strata title place, the flagperson on the road crew held her sign with the red stop side toward Cassidy's lane of traffic. When her lane finally got to creep forward, another flagperson and a big yellow sign directed them off the highway and down a side street. Halfway down that side street another big yellow sign and some blinking orange lights set into what looked like overgrown sawhorses sent them off on yet another street.

Fifteen minutes of stop-and-start go-and-wait and she wasn't any closer to the new development than she had been when she'd been stopped by that first flagperson. If anything, she was farther away. In her former life, Cassidy would have stayed in the lineup dutifully and obediently, trusting that those in charge knew what they were doing and had the very best detour route possible planned and set up for the unwary. But today she was someone else. Someone with new teeth. She set her new teeth and swung out of the lineup, drove up a side street not marked as part of the detour, and headed up a fairly steep hill. Then she turned left onto another street and drove along slowly, enjoying the view, giving up on the idea of the strata title, the appointment, the architect-designed modular units she was now convinced came out of over-grown sausage machines.

The steep hill up had taken her to the old part of town, the part some people called The Ramparts. Cassidy knew this area. To her left, the ocean; to her right, the mountains; and spread out in front of her, the roofs and backyards of houses, the pattern of streets, avenues, roads and alleys, the play-grounds and parks and, not far away, two natural lakes where migrating waterfowl stopped twice a year, some of them staying to nest and raise their young.

She hadn't been here recently, in fact she hadn't been here for a long long time. She'd grown up down there, in the valley. If she put her mind to it she could probably pick out the roof of the old place. She'd come up here to the bigger houses, to dream, to wish, to marvel at how some people managed to keep their yards clean and trimmed. Up here wasn't where the workies lived, this was where the supervi-sors and doctors lived, in big houses which became apart-ment houses almost overnight, with walls thrown up to cut lovely big houses into anthills with four or even six rental units in each place. The supervisors moved on to the new waterfront view modernities, the doctors and lawyers retired and moved to smaller places, usually on the water, where they could walk to the marina where their boats were kept.

Places like the one in which Cassidy had spent too much of her life.

Gentrification had hit this area. The huge old houses had been emptied of renters, the too-small and poorly installed apartments had been gutted, buildings that had been covered over with plywood because they were too old-fashioned were now restored. Some of the places even had little "heritage" plaques on the front. One such had a small, tasteful, businesslike Open House sign beneath the plaque, so, since Cassidy was supposed to be out looking at places, she parked on the street and went to see what there was to see.

The realtor waiting to greet the crowd, which seemed to have neglected to arrive, looked bored until he saw Cassidy peering around uncertainly. Cassidy thought later he was probably one of the juniors, and this babysitting was part of his initiation, his hell week. He looked about old enough to stop at the corner store on his way home from work and buy two or three big packs of Dubble Bubble gum.

When he realized she hadn't wandered in off the street by accident, he hit full gear immediately. Cassidy could see the visions of sugar plums dancing behind his eyes. If someone would only buy one of these damn things he might even be able to stop at the bank instead of the corner store.

She let him give her the full patter, the strata title thing and the part about the person who would do the upkeep, clean the gutters, rake the leaves from the lawn, all the things Cassidy had once done. She could have stopped him, but she didn't want him to feel cheated.

She did manage to let him know she wouldn't buy anything on the bottom floor so don't even bother showing it to her. "People," she said clearly, "will insist on trying to come over the balcony and into the apartment to swipe things."

He gave her an odd look. Heavens, did he think that was how she made her money?

"Second floor?" He sounded hesitant.

"I'd rather the top," she decided. "I'm not saying I'm buying, I haven't even seen the place, but if I was to be interested I think it would be the top floor." To him she looked about twice as old as Methuselah, and so doddery she might crumble at any sad minute. But, for crying in the night, there was a small elevator, why had they bothered installing it if not for people to use?

She liked the windows. Three sides of windows. She thought of them as chuck window, slope window and valley window. The balcony was small, but it gave her a view of the hills and the mountain above, and she already knew from childhood experience and cherished memory what the sunsets could be.

The kitchen was almost big enough for her to open a box of cereal and pour some into a bowl. The bathroom was tasteful, actually pretty, but if you spent very much time there, you'd suffocate. There were phone booths at the airport which were bigger. The main bedroom was a decent size, but what was supposed to be the second one was a joke. It was the main living area on which the attention had been focussed. Well, she thought, already feeling defensive and proprietary, why not? A person would spend the majority of her time in it. Might as well have a modest bedroom, you're sound asleep in it most of the time, and when you think of it, what are the reasons a person goes into a bathroom in the first place? How much view and ambiance does a person need to answer bodily needs? Huge numbers of people do the job on bare hillsides, without even a leaf.

Of course the attention was focussed on the main living

area. Maybe we should all focus more attention on our living areas. Especially our inner ones.

"Dear me," she murmured, and the young realtor looked at her. She thought he looked worried but she wasn't sure. Did he think he had a doddering old biddy who had somehow slipped away from the Alzheimer's clinic? She wanted suddenly to explain to him why she had said Dear me, but she couldn't remember—God, maybe she *had* slipped away from an Alzheimer's clinic! She almost giggled, but restrained herself because the poor little guy might run shrieking from the apartment, zip down the stairs without waiting for the elevator and race off down the road sobbing, leaving her alone here to conduct the Open House tours. Which she'd have to do, otherwise his career would be totally ruined and it would be all her fault.

"It's very . . . *blond*, isn't it?" She looked at him and he nodded. Something between them relaxed.

"Have to change the car you're driving, get yourself something sporty and flashy," he agreed. "Maybe get one of those big filmy scarf things to wear over your head when you're driving."

"I like the windows and all the light they let in. Doesn't seem so small a place, somehow. Mind you, nothing they do can alter the fact it isn't a large place."

"Less dust buggers. My place is smaller now. When I first started making some money and wasn't sort of going hand-to-mouth as a starving student, I dove into this big place, you'd have thought it came out of a bachelor pad magazine. Cost a lot too. I mean a *lot*. Then I had to spend more money to hire someone to come in and keep it clean. I don't know how it got so messy, I was hardly ever there. Finally decided the more room I had to make a mess, the more mess I'd make, so

I moved to a smaller place, then moved to the one I'm in. It's a bit smaller than this. And there's plenty of room. It's that thing my grandma used to talk about. Space, and whether it's used or wasted." He started to point things out to her, things she hadn't noticed, and she realized the boy really did know his business.

Cassidy was all geared up for a debate from her daughters. After all, for years, even decades, nothing she had thought of buying had been allowed to go unquestioned, unchallenged or uncriticized. Everything had to be approved, as if he and he alone knew the value of things, the worth of things, the acceptability of them. It was a surprise when her decision was met only with smiles and an eager "Can we see it?" Everyone agreed it was a lovely place, with excellent views, and they assured her and each other that she would be very comfortable there.

All this time she'd given almost no thought to Michael. She knew he'd been arrested, she knew there had been papers for her to sign, assault charges to be laid, legalities to monitor as they plodded ritually from arcane step to step, but she had thought very little about it, and not at all during the time she'd been asleep. Cori insisted on saying "comatose" but Cassidy didn't feel she'd been in a coma at all, just in a deep, restful, healing sleep. On some level she was dimly aware Michael had appeared before the court, bail had been posted and met, and he had been let out of cells. She supposed there had been long meetings with his lawyer, and probably longer secret meetings with his lawyer's wife, but she had preferred not to spend a moment of her new time thinking about him, certainly not remembering him.

But no sooner was she moved into her own place, surrounded by her new furniture, than the dreams started. At first they were not unpleasant. She dreamed of that time before she and Michael were married, when she was the courted one, the one who could not believe her luck because surely there hadn't been any reason to expect she would meet so nice a man, so different from the men she had known all her short life. Michael never sat with a long-necked brown bottle of beer, his bare feet sticking out the bottom of his faded jeans, his bare chest exposed, flaunting all that hair in the face of the world. Michael didn't even wear faded jeans. The few times he wore jeans they were almost brand new, still dark blue, still stiff. Even in the summertime he wore white shirts—the only difference between them and the ones he wore in winter was the length of the sleeves. He didn't growl or show up with three days of unshaven beard, his fingernails were always clean and short-clipped, and he didn't chew gum, let alone snoose or plug tobacco. How could she not lose her mind and fall over the edge of the world, ready to turn herself inside out to please him?

Their wedding was quiet and, at the time, she thought it was her idea. His parents couldn't make it, he said, the trip was too long, neither of them was feeling well, there would be lots of time to visit later on. Just her and Michael, her brother Tim, and two witnesses, friends of his, she thought, although it turned out later they weren't really friends at all, just people from the firm. Michael had few friends of any kind and no close ones. They didn't have a big reception, which was just as well because every wedding reception Cassidy had attended in her family had turned into the next best thing to a two-day wonder of a drunken brawl. She had expected they would visit Michael's parents as part of the honeymoon, but they didn't have one, unless you count two nights in a motel by the side of the highway. And during the day they

moved their stuff from their separate apartments into the one
they had rented to share together.

She kept her job, and hurried home after work to start
preparing supper. While it cooked she whizzed around the
apartment, tidying, dusting, vacuuming, making sure everything was Just So for Michael when he arrived. She thought
she was happy. She thought they were happy. She thought
she would learn to enjoy sex, that eventually she would stop
feeling that to Michael it didn't matter if she was there or not,
as long as the basic necessity was there.

And then she proudly announced she was pregnant. He
just stared at her, and in the same tone of voice a normal
person would use for a prayer, he said, "Oh, you fool," as if it
were some weird cerebral decision she had made all on her
own for no reason other than to inconvenience him. From
then on, nothing she did was right. The simplest things were
done incompletely, incompetently or just plain wrong.

The first slap hurt her more than anything else in her life
had hurt, more than falling from her bike into the blackberry
patch, more than jamming her finger in the car door, more
than she could have believed anything could hurt.

When the dreams got to that part, the scared part, the
resentful and angry part, she tried to turn them off. Cori insisted the dreams weren't a bad thing. After all, she said, none of
this crap surfaces until we have in ourselves everything we
need to deal with it. If you couldn't deal with it, your mind
would keep it tightly locked where it's been for all this time.
Cassidy hoped Cori was right. To her it didn't feel as if she had
everything she needed to deal with the dreams, which
seemed more and more like nightmares. But she kept reminding herself that if she had lived through the reality, she could
live through this other. Besides, there were all those people

on TV talking learnedly about false memory and how the things people remembered were often nothing more or less than fairy tales, without the happy endings, of course. She supposed for some people it must be God's own blessing to be told what they remembered hadn't happened so there was no need for them to be upset or to remain driven crazier than nits, they could just get better and get on with life. Certainly that was what she was trying to do. Get on with life.

She took long walks in the valley, often surprised at how little things had changed. She had grown up here, and maybe all the farms had gone, the meadows and pastures turned into housing developments, the big old fruit trees cut down and replaced with ornamental shrubs and blacktop parking lots, but the landmarks were there—the big old farmhouses might have been white-painted and cedar-sided and "gentrified" into apartment buildings with pricey rents, but they were still there, and it wasn't hard to ignore the row housing which had sprung up like mushrooms where the clover and orchard grass had once grown. Even when old houses had been ripped apart and broken to bits and the bits burned, the half-acre lots become the site of duplexes and triplexes, it was easy to use her mental eraser and remember when Betty McAllister lived here and had rabbits in her backyard, and Hugh McCall had lived in a big brown house on the hill with his laughing mother, noisy father and all those brothers and sisters. Hugh had a medium-sized dog, white with black patches, with Mr. Terrier having played a big part in his ancestry. The dog hated rats. All Hughie had to do was point and hiss "Rats, Scamper, rats!" and the dog would start digging. Cassidy remembered some of the holes, and the jokes the kids made about starting their own gold mining company with Scamper as their mining crew.

In the evenings she would sit on her sundeck watching the sky change colours, and she had no idea what she thought of at those times. She wondered if maybe she fell asleep, because it was as if one minute the sky was barely streaked with sunset and the next, in the blink of her eyes, it would be that dark salmon red with long purple-black streaks, the colours so intense she wanted to weep. And then poof, the gentle black rose from the slopes, and the first stars were visible. Sunset took longer than that, it was sometimes two hours between the first streaks and the final glory. So where had she been in between? Was she sliding back into what Cori insisted on calling a fugue? And wasn't a fugue some type of music?

She went into the apartment when the blackness was settling. She felt chilled and yawned often. She made tea and took it with her to the sofa she had found in the secondhand store, a sofa *he* would have insisted she take to the dump. But she loved it, even if the original cushions had become so lumpy and ugly she'd had to replace them with thick foam ones, and she couldn't find any of the original deep wine-coloured material to cover them with, so had to go in the opposite direction and find something which contrasted totally. She didn't know it was becoming very stylish to resurrect old things and she wouldn't have cared if she had known. All she knew was she felt cradled when she settled herself on her chosen chesterfield. She turned on the TV and covered herself with the shades-of-blue afghan she had made for herself. How many of the damn things had she turned out over the years without having had one for herself? Well, now she had not one, but several. She could cover the walls with them if she wanted.

The program on channel 3 was one of those ones where

the hostess seems to be in a perpetual state of flabbergasted excitement. Re-enactments figured large, with actors chosen from talentless little theatre groups. Occasionally the adrenalized hostess would interview the actual people, someone who had a poltergeist in the attic, or the woman in Ontario who lost her grandmother's engagement ring down the basin drain in the bathroom and six years later found it in the gut of a diseased fish she had caught. That was interesting, even if it was just urban myth, but the one about the hail in Port Alice was a bit goofy. They tried to re-enact the event using ping pong balls, and the silly things bounced and skittered off the hoods of cars and pick-up trucks and looked more like plastic than they would have done if they'd been in a segment about the plant which manufactured them. Cassidy laughed so hard at the sight of all those ping pong balls bouncing in the lawn that she thought she would spill her tea.

And then there it was, on TV, the image of the house in which she had spent so many years of her life. There was no sign of Michael. Well, of course, he wouldn't be caught dead getting interviewed by this program! They were talking about the rain. About how the rain had first begun months earlier, and they interviewed the police who had investigated, interviewed even the waterworks inspector and the plumbers. They had to use zoom lenses to get shots of the door and the steps because obviously Michael had refused them permission to set foot on the place, but even so you could see water seeping from beneath the front door, oozing across the porch and trickling down the steps to the sidewalk. In a state of permanent agitation the hostess went on at great length about how the first manifestation had stopped and the house had been—at great expense, she assured the world—cleaned and dried. And then the rain had started again, and nothing anybody did could stop it, nor could any explanation be found for it.

Because they couldn't go in the house they tried a studio re-enactment, but they had it all wrong. It didn't look like the inside of Michael's house at all, and the rain they faked wasn't the least bit like the rain which had fallen. On TV it looked as if they had just turned on an overhead sprinkler.

She phoned Cori and asked her if she had known it was raining inside Michael's house again.

"Yes," Cori said, sounding as if she almost wished Cassidy hadn't found out. "I knew. Father is furious. He can't live in the house and now he can't sell it, either, because everything is drenched and starting to mildew."

"If he's not in the house, where is he? In a hotel?"

"No, Mother." Cori sounded tired. "He's in jail again."

"Nobody told me!"

"Nobody wanted to upset you. When the water started in the house again he got upset, called the police, didn't like what they said to him, so he punched one of them in the nose. They arrested him and the judge said maybe he should stay in jail until his court appearance next week."

"Dear me."

"Dear me, indeed. All of a sudden he seems to think we should all take a hand and 'Be there for him.' If I've had one phone call from his lawyer, I've had ten. I'm about ready to rip the phone from the wall. I would, but then the hospital wouldn't be able to get hold of me."

"You aren't thinking, dear. You do have a beeper."

"Right, and it would go off and I'd respond and it would be the damn lawyer!"

The program was ending, and the screen was flashing all those bits of images which meant the evening movie was about to start. Cassidy refilled her mug with tea, added honey, adjusted the afghan, and settled back to enjoy it. It was exactly the kind of movie Michael would have refused to watch. Even when he wasn't watching TV he felt free to censor the programs. She wondered why it was necessary for some people to get total control over the lives of other people. Then she wondered why there were so many people like her, handing over control so easily.

Michael's trial did not slip by unnoticed as so many do. Michael's trial hit the front page. Cassidy found herself thinking sourly that if more such trials were front page news there might be less need for so many of them.

But it wasn't because of Michael, because of what he had done, because of what he was charged with doing, or the sentence he got that made the whole thing such a big deal. It was the rain in the jail was the big news. This time there was no need for low-budget fakey re-enactments. The authorities willingly let the news crews in to shoot miles of film of the rain coming from the ceiling, or maybe through the ceiling, nobody was ever exactly sure where the rain originated. All the cells were flooded, the computers in the administration office were ruined, all the prisoners had to be moved to what had been the old high school, with extra staff hired to keep them there. The jail itself was under twenty-four-hour observation, the guards looking more like fishers or coast guard workers in heavy rain gear and knee-high rubber boots. One of the reporters remembered trying to cover the story of the flooded house and the rain everyone said was falling inside it, and realized Michael was the link between the two bizarre, unbelievable, freakish events. That's how Michael's trial wound up in the headlines of first the local, then the provincial, and very quickly the national news. He wouldn't have enjoyed such exposure. But then it couldn't affect him much any more, he'd lost his job when he got tossed in the pokey the second time, for punching the policeman in the nose.

As part of the ongoing journalistic wonder, someone unearthed a picture of Cassidy taken six months or so before she wound up in her fugue. Someone else bribed someone, either at the hospital or at the police detachment, and other pictures were published showing Cassidy's face at the time she was hospitalized. Another time, another set of circumstances, and she would have been livid at the invasion of privacy, but now it didn't matter a whit to her. Nobody was going to recognize that exhausted looking woman, nobody was going to look at Cassidy now and think, That's the poor drudge got her lights punched out. Even Cassidy hardly recognized the pictures of her old self. When she looked in her mirror she saw only who she was now—hair white as snow, or, more like it, silver; eyes clear and too blue to be true. You could see hints of where the lines had been in her face, but the deep-cut worry grooves were gone from between her brows, from the corners of her mouth. She had crow's feet at her eyes, but they were hardly noticeable, especially when she smiled. She could walk down the main street of town, past the newspaper boxes where those pictures of her were displayed, and not a living soul paid any attention. She even showed up in court and sat in the spectator section without anyone recognizing her.

She didn't have to testify in person because Michael had caved in and pleaded no contest to the charges. The judge seemed to sleep through the hurried presentation of evidence, then sentenced Michael to six weeks. He couldn't send him to jail because the jail was flooded, so instead he ordered Michael to wear an electronic device around his ankle and stay in his apartment under house arrest. Cassidy thought it was funny they called it house arrest when it wasn't a house at all, and she thought six weeks was the next best thing to nothing at all, but she supposed that her getting pounded to a pulp was a more significant event in her life than in the lives of the officials.

What she enjoyed most was the look on Michael's face when he realized who she was. He stared. He just kept staring, and Cassidy couldn't help feeling a deep satisfaction. Michael looked a wreck. Oh, his suit was as tickety-boo as ever, his shirt as white and as starched, his maroon tie knotted just exactly so, his shoes shined. All the stuff was there, but he himself looked as if he'd been dragged backwards through a firethorn hedge. She half expected him to argue with the judge about the sentence, and was disappointed when all he did was nod, looking as if he looked forward to spending the entire six weeks sleeping.

And then it began to rain in the courtroom. The judge pounded his little wooden hammer, but that didn't stop the fine drizzle. The security guards climbed on chairs to check the overhead sprinklers, but they weren't malfunctioning. The judge yelled "Order, order!" but there wasn't any, the spectators were all jumping to their feet, asking each other what was going on, talking about the flooded jail and the sodden house, while Michael just sat there, his suit getting wetter and wetter, his white shirt wilting, his shoes losing their shine.

Cassidy got up and left. Her shoes were wet, her ankle-length skirt was wet, her brightly coloured blouse was wet and her silver hair glistened, the water droplets catching the

light and twinkling like diamonds. The last thing she heard
was the judge shouting that someone better find out what all
this was about.

The newspapers and TV started to refer to Michael as Joe
Bzltfyk, that famous Joe Gloom character, and a local
cartoonist drew a picture of Michael sitting under a black
cloud, rain falling on his head. When the TV showed him
leaving the courthouse, clothes dripping, the background
music they played was "Raindrops Keep Falling on My Head,"
and little kids threw pennies on the sidewalk in front of his
apartment building while screeching Every time it rains it
rains pennies from heaven.

Six weeks isn't much. Six weeks is really nothing at all.
The thought of six weeks burned like fury in Cassidy's soul.
She felt as if the court had done the same thing Michael had
done, that once again she had been whacked and walloped.
She wondered if things would have been different if Michael
had gone up in front of a woman judge, and then decided
nothing would have been different unless the woman judge
had herself been a battered wife. She started going to the
library and checking out books of a kind Michael would never
have allowed her to read, books written by women he would
have called Feminazis, books which shocked her, threatened
her and, eventually, satisfied her. Often she wanted to write to
the authors to argue with them, to say No, it isn't like that at
all, and a couple of times she actually started letters she knew
she wouldn't mail but felt she had to write anyway. Halfway
through them she knew *she* wasn't the one who was dis-
agreeing, it was just her conditioning, her training, her edu-
cation and upbringing that needed to argue, to deny.

She hardly saw anybody. One or the other of her daughters would phone every day, and she could have eaten every

meal with them, but she wanted and needed to be alone in her apartment. She didn't know why. She couldn't have explained it. She loved them almost obsessively, she just wanted to be alone. She walked for long hours every day, ignoring the newness around her and concentrating on what had been, trying to figure out how she had wound up where she had been before it started to rain. At night she dreamed of water, heaving waves with sun dancing on the surface. Sometimes it seemed in her dream as if she were looking at the world from just above the surface of the water, as if she were completely submerged except for her eyes. Other times she might have been sprawled on a sun-drenched rock, wavelets lapping at her feet, her body warm and dry. Other times she dreamed she could see the *Shoes for the Baby*, see Mikey and Tim on deck, working incredibly hard, clearing nets. More than once she saw them bring from the webbing a dogfish, already drowned; they threw it over the side and seals barked thanks. Mikey grinned at them and waved, and Cassidy, in the water with just her eyes above the surface, wanted to wave back, call greeting.

The day Michael's six-week sentence was finished, the TV news had pictures of him going into the courthouse to have his little monitor bracelet taken from his ankle. His clothes were wet and he looked as if he had lost forty pounds and missed entire nights of sleep. Cassidy supposed she ought to feel sorry for him, but she didn't. The following night there he was, in the studio with the anchorman, subject of what they promised would be an in-depth interview. She was so insulted, so enraged, she didn't even hear the first couple of questions. Were they going to turn him into some kind of media star? Would they pay for him to travel first class to appear on *Donahue*? Would Oprah pick up the tab for a fancy hotel and gourmet meals just so this twerp could go around trying to make people feel sorry for him? Was she going to be haunted forever by his image on her TV set, his picture in the newspaper, his face staring blankly from magazine covers?

He sat in the studio looking suitably humble, even cha-grined, and she just knew there were people out there who felt that the poor guy had suffered enough, even too much. The anchorman kept reminding people the scientists were baffled, the police were unable to even begin to explain, the Pope had issued a statement declaring how mysterious the ways of God were, and the Queen had promised something, Cassidy couldn't remember what. A government inquiry had already begun, and medical specialists at the university wanted to attach electrodes and wires to Michael's head and monitor his brain wave activity to see if they could find, or invent, a reason for what they called The Phenomenon.

So much attention! As if sitting in a recurrent rain were something wonderful. As if it proved in some way what Michael had believed most of his life—that he was indeed made in the image of God, and thus nearly godlike.

Cassidy got so mad she reached for the phone to call the station and protest, but before she could get the number dialled, rain started to fall inside the TV studio. Not just a fine mist or drizzle, an all-out pelting rain. The effect was immedi-ate. The anchorman jumped from his seat, trailing wires, the camera people scrambled to protect their treasured tech-nology, people ran to cover banks of electronic gear and, before the microphones were turned off, the watching audi-ence was treated to such gems as Jesus Christ what next, and Get this bugger out of here before the place is wrecked.

The screen went blank momentarily, and then a taped article about forest fires in Idaho popped on. When that item was finished the screen showed the studio again. A different anchorperson, one with dry clothes, stood in front of the camera. She looked flustered and uncertain, but determined to do her best. She apologized for the technical difficulties and promised the in-depth interview would continue later in the program.

When it did, Michael was standing on the lawn outside the TV station, with the original anchorman. They were standing under a huge beach umbrella bearing advertising for Martini & Rossi, and the sound of the water hitting the canvas was so loud they both had to shout to be heard. Even then their words were almost inaudible. The camera pulled back for a medium-distance shot and there they were, two men in suits, under a big umbrella, standing in a column of rain. The sky was clear, and fifty feet in any direction the air and everything else was dry, but above them the torrent poured.

Cassidy giggled. No way was anyone going to be able to make a hero out of Michael, not even a weird eccentric one. He looked like a fool and the TV anchorman interviewing him looked like an idiot. People all across the country were laughing. Laughing scornfully. The two-man goon show, their wet clothes sticking to them, the starch in their shirts dissolving. She laughed until her own face was wet with tears, then stepped out on her balcony to watch the sunset.

Just before she went to sleep that night she thought of Idaho, and the forest fires, and all those poor animals trying to flee to safety. She tried to remember where exactly Idaho was. Somewhere next to Washington state, she thought. Or maybe Oregon. Over there under Alberta, near Montana. They grew spuds there, and maybe corn. She hadn't thought there was enough forest left in Idaho to fuel a good fire, but she had seen the pictures on TV, so it must be true. Poor bear trying to get cubby to safety. Poor squirrel hearing her babies screaming with agony as their tree-home was devoured. And what about the flickers and woodpeckers? She could have wept but she was so sleepy. So very very sleepy.

She didn't turn on the TV until the next day at noon. They didn't re-run the catastrophic interview with Michael, in fact they all seemed determined to forget it ever happened. They did, however, announce to the waiting world that a sudden and unpredicted rainstorm had drenched Washington, Oregon, Idaho and Montana. Fields were flooded, bridges washed out, roads closed, and the huge forest fire had been not only brought under control but virtually extinguished. Cassidy breathed a sigh of relief. See, she thought, sometimes there is so a bit of good news on TV. And they probably wouldn't dare try to iconize the batterer again. Not with their technology at risk.

But someone had decided it was time to interview the wife. Cassidy tried to insist she wasn't the wife, she was the ex-wife. But the divorce hadn't gone through and anyway they wanted the wife and that was how they were going to write it. Cassidy wasn't interested in being interviewed. It annoyed her that she had to disconnect her phone, it angered her that she had to have her door buzzer turned off, and it choked her up that she couldn't leave her apartment without someone ramming a foam-covered microphone practically up her nose. She was so sick of saying "No comment" that she felt like yelling *Fuck off* instead, and would have done except it would only have encouraged them. Inside twenty-four hours there would have been twice as many of them.

So she just climbed in her car and took off. No suitcase, no backpack, nothing but a toothbrush and a tube of tooth-paste stuck in her jacket pocket. She didn't want them to know she was going out for anything other than an ice cream cone at the corner store.

She let Cori know she was leaving and Cori promised to tell Maria and Liberty and Freedom. There was no way to tell Mikey until she radiophoned home, but Mikey wouldn't worry too much anyway.

– V –

Cassidy had no idea where she was going, she just knew she wasn't going to sit in her apartment, under siege. They had taken a number of photos of her as she was now, and for a while she feared her anonymity was gone, she would be accosted on the street, unable to find any place where she could wait out the wonder of it all. Surely the whole thing would fade away. Surely even if it didn't stop raining on Michael, something else would come up on which the media could fixate. After all, what kind of big deal was it? A bit of unexplained rain. Why was that on the front page of every paper in the world when millions of Africans were dying, war was trying to break out in amazing numbers of countries, and the fish stocks of both the Atlantic and Pacific were at endangered levels?

Photos or not, no one pays attention to a woman with silvery-white hair. The best possible disguise for a contract killer would be to appear as a middle-aged or older woman. Just grow his hair, bleach it, shave his beard and legs and dress himself in women's clothing. He could move around unnoticed, unremarked and unacknowledged forever.

She didn't do anything earth-shattering. She just drove to places she had thought she might like to visit one day, and visited them. The only thing that puzzled her in the least was her purse and the money in it. When she had taken the money she knew exactly how much of it there was. And when she added up what she'd spent for her condo and the furniture, some new, some secondhand, she was sure she had put out more than she'd originally had. And yet whenever she reached into her purse, there was money. Never a lot, not buckets of it, her purse wasn't big enough to hold a bucket of anything. A few fifties, a few twenties, and whatever change she'd got from her last purchase. It was completely puzzling and made her think of the old story of the loaf of bread which was never fully eaten, the block of cheese which renewed itself, the flagon of wine which was never empty. She thought it all very convenient.

From various flickering television sets in various roadside motels, Cassidy knew that Michael wasn't finding anything very convenient. The superintendent of the apartment building had made him move to the laundry room in the basement, where there was a drain in the concrete floor. "It's going to take weeks to dry the apartment," he ranted on TV, "and it's cost a fortune. The gyproc walls have to be replaced, the ceiling is ruined, and the apartment directly beneath him on the floor below is soaked too. In the laundry room he can rain on himself to his heart's content and it can all run out the floor drain." They even had pictures of Michael sitting on a small bed, an umbrella propped beside him, trying to read a magazine. He was wearing a Speedo bathing suit and little rubber beach shoes, and when he looked up and saw the camera operator in the doorway he didn't even speak, let alone shout and holler.

She visited salmon hatcheries and game farms, she saw waterfalls and hydroelectric projects, she sat on beaches and watched cormorants, seals and otters, and she thought about her life, and what little she knew of the lives of other people. Something seemed just a fraction out of whack. If you're walking down the road and you turn off it and start down an alleyway, as soon as you realize it doesn't go anywhere you can just turn around, go back, get your feet back on the right road and continue, having lost only a minute or two. But you can't do that with your life. You make a choice and even if it's a misguided split-second decision, that's it. The right road, or what you've been taught is the right road, might be in sight, it might be just over there, in clear view, but you aren't on it any more and you never will be again. In her case it was two words, *I do*, and she wasn't out there with what they called the mainstream at all, she was picking up baggage, and even if the baggage turned out to be two wonderful daughters, and even if she loved them extravagantly and couldn't imagine life without them, she was on a different path, and the longer she stayed on it, the less chance of keeping that other road, the right road, in sight.

What had happened to all those girls she had known in school? What paths had they taken? Had any of them managed to stay on the right road, making what they had all been taught were the proper choices? And how had they all lost touch with each other? My God, they had grown up together, some of them had been dearer to her than her own siblings. Their lives were completely entangled—to a point, and then after that point, there were just ever-widening blanks.

She wished her mother were still alive so they could sit with a pot of tea and some toasted English muffins, with raspberry jam and small pieces of marbled cheese, and talk for a little while. Really talk, not spar with each other or fall into that awful conversational trap they'd been in for so long, with each of them pretending to listen politely but really just waiting until the other finished her monologue so the other could begin hers. Two people, two monologues, and no dialogue. Maybe what she wanted wasn't so much to talk to her mother as to have one last chance to listen and be listened to, to hear and be heard.

But she doubted either of them would ever have listened or heard. By the time she figured it out, it was too late, the habit was too deeply entrenched. Had her mother ever felt as desperate to communicate as Cassidy had? She hoped so. How could two people who knew each other so well, lived in the same house, ate the same food, shared the same acquaintances, wind up speaking what might as well have been two different languages? They would try to talk and entire concepts would whiz past each other's heads. Maybe it was better the way it was. Maybe she could walk the beach and imagine conversations, make her point, tell her tale, get her message across in a way she had never been able to do when her mother was still alive.

She had never yearned to talk to her father. She would never sit on a sun-bleached log at the edge of a wild sea and imagine healing conversations with him. She didn't call him back, even in memory. She'd spent too many decades piling dirt on his grave, making sure he was well and truly interred. If she hadn't been afraid of the law and jail and rah rah rah she'd have driven a wooden stake into the ground and kept pounding on it until she was certain it had gone through the dirt, the coffin lid, the satin lining and the old fart's heart. All this karma stuff people talk about and wouldn't you think, if even it was true, that a soul or a spirit would *know*, for Chrissakes, what the living were like and then be smart enough not to choose to be born to wing nuts? People out praying and baying at the moon and doing ritual and the goddess alone knows what to call on the spirits to help them, and the spirits seem to be just a tad idiotic, so many of them are choosing to come back and ride the karmic wheel again, with lunatics for parents.

She stopped for lunch at an oysterburger stand and that's where she saw the notice on a bulletin board. Zodiac charters. All she had to do was make a phone call and someone would take her out for a ride in a big rubber boat. She was promised the chance to see otter and sea lions, possibly even a whale or two. It sounded wonderful. It was at least one of those side paths or alleys she hadn't already tried and had to turn back. She'd never been in a Zodiac, she'd never been near a wild seal or seen a real sea lion. She'd watched enough wildlife programs to know they had bad breath and a strong fishy stink in general, but was she going to go to her grave knowing no more than that?

She met the operator at the dock at the appointed time. She had a big stainless steel thermos of coffee and several sandwiches she had bought at the supermarket deli, also a few Mars bars and a spare package of cigarettes, all carefully placed in a brand new purple backpack. She had her purse in the backpack as well, and a spare sweater, a heavy hand-knit one made of pure wool.

The operator was probably no older than thirty-five, with darkly tanned skin, sun-bleached blond hair and a wide grin. He helped her step from the dock into the Zodiac and handed her a life jacket. She put it on, zipped it shut and did up the straps, then settled herself, her pack slung on her back. She had to undo the webbing straps and move them to the very end before it would fit over her life jacket. It made her feel a bit off balance but there was a fine film of water on the bottom of the rubber boat and she didn't much feel like lunching on brine-soaked egg salad sandwiches.

She had expected to be the only passenger but there were six other people, obviously three couples, and though she smiled at them and nodded, she was disappointed. She knew they would oooooh and aaaaaah and talk to each other, and she wanted silence. Besides, they made her feel out of place, not just because they were in couples and holding hands, even snuggling, but because there she was, in Nike high-tops, thick cotton socks, jeans and a warm sweatshirt, and there they were in shorts, sandals and bright-coloured tee shirts. Of course they were already goose-pimpled and only pretending to be comfortable, especially when the breeze blew, but once again she didn't fit what the majority had decided was the norm. How are these decisions made, anyway? Is it some kind of herd instinct, like lemmings racing across miles of open tundra? Or do they meet in secret to discuss, then vote? And if so why had nobody ever notified her of the time and place of the meeting? There was no use asking them. If she did, they'd give her The Look. Then inch away from her as if whatever she had was contagious.

The Zodiac sped across the surface of the choppy sea, and within five minutes Cassidy was glad she hadn't been invited to the meeting, hadn't been bound by the decision to come togged up like tourists in a tropical paradise. The wind was stiff, and this close to the water it was cold, and the spray coming over the front of the Zodiac was as close to ice as water could get and still be liquid. The sun-worshippers were shivering so hard Cassidy almost pulled her spare sweater out of her pack and offered it, but which one should she give it to? There were three women and there was no way they could share. She started to worry about them and then gave herself a good shaking. After all, she had expected to come alone and she had wanted to come alone, and if she kept her back turned to them she could pretend she *was* alone. She wasn't their mother, and anyway if even one of them had the sense to tell the operator to go back so they could get warmer clothes, the operator would turn back at once. But not one of them spoke to the operator, they just nattered to each other. Their voices annoyed Cassidy but she just tuned them out.

The sky was blue, the ocean was blue, it was hard to tell where one stopped and the other started. The whitecaps could have been bits of broken cloud and it wouldn't take any effort at all to imagine they were flying. Cassidy wondered what lived down there, below the surface of the waves, peeping just over the surface as she had done in her dreams. Did mammoth sea monsters move slowly through the depths, their mouths open like traps, harvesting krill or plankton? Did huge creatures prowl through the waves, eating pilchard and herring, cod and salmon? All her life she'd heard stories about Cadborosaurus, the sea monster who was said to have at least six humps, a snaky neck, a doglike head and long tendrils of what was either hair or antennae. Some people said this beast was the cousin of the Loch Ness monster, most called it "Caddy," and some referred to it as Cadborosaurus Rex, but Cassidy had always thought it a Regina. Did it really exist and was it even now snoozing beneath them? Or was it swimming, and was it the lazy motion of its gigantic fins caused the waves to heave? *It* swimming? No. *Her* swimming. Was *she* swimming, and was it the lazy motion of *her* gigantic fins caused the waves to heave?

There was no doubt the waves were heaving. The complaints and ohmigawdiflhadonlyknownl'dhavewornheavier-clothes litanies from the six sitting behind her had stopped, and the only sounds they made now were little gasps and moans of fear. And still, not one of them had the sense to ask the operator to turn around and go back. Maybe the men were afraid to ask in case their testicles withered and dropped off, to lie exposed in the gathering water on the bottom of the boat, floating like little prunes. And maybe the women, by now half frozen and all terrified, hadn't said anything because they were passively waiting for the men, or maybe they were like Cassidy used to be, terrified of saying anything, knowing the trouble would somehow be construed as her fault, knowing they'd be well punished for it later. Well, if no one else would ask to turn back, Cassidy would. Let them blame the little old white-haired lady.

She leaned forward and tapped the operator on the shoulder. He turned and smiled. Cassidy tried to speak and couldn't. Where had the good-looking young blond man gone? Somehow he had been replaced by this sinister-looking ageless man with sleek dark hair. Somehow the bright blue eyes had been replaced by these round, dark ones, so dark it seemed as if they were all pupil, holes into which your soul could plummet and be lost for eternity. He smiled at Cassidy and she knew there was no use suggesting they go back. His teeth were the sharp-pointed catlike teeth of a carnivore.

"Oh, you rotten bastard," she managed. And then the Zodiac was turning end over end, she had a glimpse of the propeller egg-beatering ineffectually at the air, and the water closed over her head.

Cassidy was furious. Jesus Christ, and to think she had actually paid money for the chance to be duped and dumped. Is there no end to the perfidy of people? What did that guy think he'd get out of this? At best, her backpack with the thermos and a few sandwiches, surely soaked and inedible by now. Her purse, yes, but did he really want a purse, and if he did why not go buy one?

She was angry with herself, too, for being such a damn fool as to pay money to sit chilled in a rubber boat with a purple backpack strapped in on top of a bright orange life preserver. She must have looked a total idiot. She must have *been* a total idiot. To pay all that money to look like a moron and then get dumped in the chuck.

She kicked her feet and fought her way to the surface, realizing at the same time that she still wore both the life jacket and the backpack. The upside-down Zodiac, probably useless by now, was a good hundred feet away from her and one of the women had managed to swim to it and grab onto what looked like a rope. She clung tightly with both hands, her mouth open, screeching wordlessly. Cassidy would willingly have swum over and joined her, wailing and howling, bellyaching and protesting, but there were too many marine mammals in the water between them. Not sea lions, and certainly not otter, these looked like seals. But the colour was wrong. The only seals Cassidy had seen, even on wildlife TV programs, were sort of silvery-grey with dark brown or black blotches on them. These wotzits were bigger than she had thought a seal would be, and their fur was a rich, dark, gorgeous brown. Some of them, in fact, seemed to be the same lovely russet colour of Liberty and Freedom's thick curly hair. Their eyes were round and black, and when they opened their mouths to bark and snarl, Cassidy saw their teeth were long, white, and very very sharp.

Something red stained the water and Cassidy was afraid she knew what it was. All the women seemed to be okay, the one still clinging to the Zodiac, the other two swimming desperately to join her. But two of the men had vanished and the third was struggling, flailing, his pale face turned to the sky, his mouth open but no sound coming from it.

That's when she remembered the stories from when she was a child. Don't tease the seals, don't throw rocks at the seals, and if the seals show up, grab hold of your dog's collar or the seals will bark and tease and challenge until the dog races into the water to confront them, and then the seals will grab the dog, dive under the water and stay there until the dog has drowned. And after that, the seals will feast. Some of the old-timers had called the seals the dogs of the sea, others had said wolves, not dogs.

And that's what they were doing now, hauling the third man down into the water, holding him there, not just one or two of them but too many to count, hanging onto him with their savage teeth, hanging off him like grapes on a vine.

Then one of them attacked the Zodiac. Not the women, but the rubber boat itself. At least six feet long, the seal came up out of the water and ripped at the inflated boat with those awful, awful teeth. Even two hundred yards away, Cassidy could hear the hiss as the boat began to deflate.

She had no idea why she was drifting away so quickly. She ought to have been moving toward the Zodiac, the waves were rolling in that direction, the wind was blowing that way. But she was moving against the forces of nature, almost as though she were being pulled. Well, leave us not quibble with small mercies, at least she was putting some distance between herself and those terrifying animals. There must have been a half dozen of them attacking the rubber boat, ripping it open compartment by compartment. The women were screaming, and small wonder. Bad enough they were losing the Zodiac, but Cassidy could see what else the seals, or whatever they were, had in mind. They surged up out of the water to slash at the boat and, even from this distance, Cassidy could see their erections. They weren't trying to bite the women, weren't trying to kill them or eat them. No withered prunes here, no four and a half inches trying to pretend to be nine. She suddenly thought of her father's idea of a joke when he was drunk, Just get it in 'er and then spin 'er.

It was too much. Cassidy's mind turned off. She couldn't possibly sort it all out, understand it, even try to believe it. She didn't have to go to the trouble of fainting, she just turned the switch, let herself give up every vestige of control, and let whatever was going on flow over her without protesting.

She was travelling backward, unable to see where she was going, able only to see where she had been. The Zodiac and the struggling women were reduced to a few dark dots on a heaving grey sea, and within minutes she couldn't see even that much. She could hear surf pounding and she supposed, with the kind of luck she'd been having lately, she would survive the initial assault only to be thrown onto jagged rocks and slashed to ribbons of macerated flesh. Give with one hand, take away with the other. If it isn't one damn thing it's another.

She wasn't macerated, she wasn't even lacerated, but she did get one hell of a whack on the head. She could feel sand and pebbles under her and she had only enough sense left to flail herself a few feet farther up onto the strand, enough that her face was clear of the water. She turned her head to one side, spat gravel and bits of broken shell from her mouth, tried to pull it all together and then had to give up and let the bang on the head do what it was going to do anyway.

She came to a few minutes later and sat up, her head pounding, her eyes blinking and overly sensitive to the light.

Her legs were cold, her feet felt like blocks of ice, and she knew she had to get out of the water into the sunlight. She also knew those wet clothes had to go or hypothermia was going to claim her.

She crawled up from the edge of the ocean, across the small rounded stones on the gravel beach, toward a cluster of large, flat black rocks. She could see heat waves rising from the rocks and she knew they were more like salvation than any church she had ever set foot in.

She fumbled at straps and zippers, dropping her backpack, discarding her life jacket, pulling off her wet, cold sweatshirt. Off with the sodden Nikes, off with the thick cotton socks, and out of the stiff, cold jeans. She had enough sense to lay them on rocks to dry, and then she eased herself belly down on the flat top of the biggest black stone, and sighed. The warmth was immediate. The warmth was better than any sex she'd ever had in her life. Not that sex had been a big number at the best of times, but it was like sex, this spreading heat, warming her from the inside out, warming her until she could feel little beads of sweat beginning to form. Out on the ocean there was no sign that there had ever been a Zodiac, three couples and an operator who transmuted seemingly at will. What had happened had been perfectly outrageous, and Cassidy supposed she should be feeling more, reacting more. But what good would it do and who would even see? There was absolutely nothing she could do, except sleep.

– VI –

When she wakened, she felt almost normal, probably because she suspected the whole thing—storm, seals,
humungous whangs and improbable metamorphoses—had
been a dream. Maybe she was still dreaming, still bobbing
safely in the little rubber boat, sleeping, possibly even snor-
ing, while the others snickered at her and whispered things
like Pay all that money for an excursion and then sleep
through the whole thing.

Her clothes were still damp, and she supposed everything
in her pack was drenched and ruined. She ought to have
checked it sooner. She climbed off the rock and, stark naked,
moved to the purple haversack. There were scratches and
even gouges on the front, she guessed from being banged or
scraped against rocks, although she had no memory of having slammed into any. It actually looked as if something . . .
something . . . had grabbed the pack with long, sharp teeth
and hauled on it. She didn't remember any of the strange
giant seals lunging at her, and if it had, she couldn't imagine
why it had let go. So it had to be rocks. Didn't it?

She opened the scarred pack and was astounded to find
its contents merely damp. Her purse was there. Her heavy
sweater was there, and only slightly moist. She took it out and

put it on the hot black rock—she would need it if this dream
continued. Her stainless steel thermos beckoned and when
she unscrewed the cap the smell of still-hot coffee was like a
blessing from the goddess herself. Amazingly, everything in
her purse was bone dry, even her cigarettes. Finally she was
convinced that yes, this was all a dream. You can't be
dumped into the chuck, bobbed and zipped around like a
cork, swept along against the tides, then marooned on a glo-
rified hump of rock and have your damn cigarettes survive.
But there they were, and when she lit one and sat on the
sand, her back against the warm rock, sipping hot coffee and
inhaling deeply, she felt so relaxed, so free she almost wished
the experience was real and she wouldn't have to wake up
when the Zodiac got back to the dock. If a person had to nod
off and dream, this was the dream to have, a dream head and
shoulders above the usual kind, the racing down the tracks
trying to outrun the train kind, the running through molasses
trying to get away from the threat kind, or that dream she
really hated where she found herself suddenly in a barn or a
shed facing unlimited numbers of rundown jerry-built cages
in which someone—who, for God's sake?!—was keeping
helpless little animals, cats with kittens or small dogs with
puppies or, most often, rabbits with bunnies. In that dream
chickens ran around hysterically, flapping up onto the cages,
squawking that awful noise that sounds so much like *Help*.
And all the defenceless little animals were starving. The
babies' eyes were too big for their bony little faces, their
noses were like little needles, their fur was patchy and they
were covered with big sores. Cassidy worked her way through
this dream frantically opening cage doors and removing animals that were nearly paralyzed, trying to get them to drink,
trying to get them to eat, and the whole time she herself was

sobbing and apologizing. Pigeons would land and coo peacefully as if things like this happened a dozen times a night, but there was no comfort in them because as calm and tranquil as they sounded, Cassidy could see only that they were infested with lice. There was never any resolution to the dream, she wakened in a sweat, feeling totally depressed, wanting to cry forever, her skin itching, her nostrils still full of the stink of dead and dying creatures.

This dream, of the seaside and the warm rocks and the quiet and the hot coffee, was so much better. Cassidy wondered if she could hypnotize herself or something, and call on this dream in the future.

Anyone with any sense would sip at the coffee, make it last, dole it out a few drops at a time, who knew if there was any drinking water on this big black hump? But why prolong the agony, and anyway, sooner or later the operator would return to the pier and shake Cassidy's shoulder until she was awake. The coffee wouldn't smell and taste so wonderful then. It would just be coffee, and thermos coffee at that.

She poured a second cup and looked for her egg salad sandwiches. Not a sign of them. Not even the waxed paper in which they had been wrapped. Now that was weird. How had they got out of the pack? Not floated out, surely, the zipper had been closed. She would have been willing to accept that the sandwiches had dissolved to pulp in the sea water, except the inside of the pack was barely damp and waxed paper doesn't dissolve. Besides, wouldn't something like that leave a layer of sodden gunk, wouldn't something like that soil and stain the sweater? She looked in the pack again. Not a crumb. An unwelcome image flashed into her mind: a huge seal, russet-furred and round-eyed, grabbing the pack with its murderous teeth, swimming away from the soon-to-be ruined

Zodiac, pulling Cassidy away from the ones with the huge badoinkeys . . . and reaching up with a flipper, unzipping the pack, happily feasting on the sandwiches *and* the Mars bars.

No. The image was too ridiculous. Seals don't eat sandwiches, and they particularly don't eat Mars bars. Maybe Cassidy hadn't put them in there after all. But of course she had! She clearly remembered doing it. Inside her skull she felt her brain swelling, struggling to solve this mystery, and she felt the familiar rising panic, oh God, now what have I done or not done, Michael will be so angry. And then the panic was gone, like a bubble which bursts silently when you poke it with your finger. Why get her knickers in a knot over a few sandwiches, especially when she wasn't even hungry!

The cigarette tasted like the first one she had ever smoked. Like something she had been born to do. She remembered that first one so clearly. All the valley kids had taken jam sandwiches and Mason jars of drinking water and walked to the lake. Anyone looking at them would have known they were kids from working poor families by the look they shared, an on-guard alertness, a distrust. They sealed their bottles of drinking water and sunk them to the bottom of the lake to keep cool. Everyone knew you didn't dare drink the lake water, there were too many cedar logs on the bottom, dumped into the lake in the days when their grandmothers were girls, rejects and discards from the first logging. They talked of how the logs must have choked the surface of the lake, filling it until there was no room for ducks to swim or kingfishers to dive, no room even for fish to surface and gulp air or bugs. And still the discards were dumped, the later ones pushing the earlier ones under the water until they began to get waterlogged, grow heavier and heavier, sink lower and lower, until eventually they were piled on the bottom. Some of the bigger boys claimed they had found big rocks, cuddled them against their chests, jumped from the bank and plunged down, down, down to where layer upon layer of cedar logs lay on top of the mud. They insisted there were so many logs down there they were stacked tight, jammed solid, in a hunk at least twenty feet thick. Cassidy had never believed they had gone that deep or been able to see so much as their hand in front of their face once they got there. And she wasn't convinced the stack was twenty feet thick, either. But still, she carried drinking water when she went there. Why be different? And how stupid would you feel if you did defy tradition and then got sick as a pig?

They ate their sandwiches and exchanged cookies, and then Ray brought out a small flat tin, a perfect size to fit in a back pocket. He opened it and started rolling a cigarette, then grinned at Cassidy. "Wanna try?" She didn't hesitate. If Ray suggested it, she was ready. If Ray had said Let's fly to the moon and then jump off into empty space, Cassidy's feet would have left the ground.

He handed her that first rollin's, and she waited until his own was ready. "Don't chickenlip it," he warned. "You only put it in your lips, not in your mouth. And don't take too big a puff at first because you aren't used to this and it can really hit you."

Her first puff was just that, a puff. She expected to cough and splutter, the way they showed it on the big movie screen at the Apollo theatre. The warm smoke slid down her throat to her lungs, and immediately she felt dizzy. When she grinned she knew it was a goofy grin, but she didn't care. She puffed again, then sighed, and that sigh relaxed places inside her she hadn't even known she had. It was as if she had spent years and years waiting anxiously for this moment, this experience. Ray smiled again and sprawled next to her on the grass beside the lake. They smoked in silence and she wanted to do something, but didn't know what, wanted to say thank you but didn't dare.

And smoking this cigarette, here, alone, on this baking islet or whatever it was, felt that same dreamy way. She supposed she ought to ration herself with them, too, but knew she wouldn't.

Where was Ray now? She hadn't seen him or heard a word about him for years, many years. The last she had heard, he'd been married, divorced, married a second time, separated, and was shacked up with someone. Along the line he'd fathered seven kids. Well, seven kids the last time she'd heard about him. Who knew how many by now?

The coffee and cigarette worked the same magic on her that they did every morning, they kick-started her brain. Before long she was thinking of something more important and more immediate than old crushes and first smokes. She looked around her, wondering what she could use for shelter. Obviously she was going to be here all night, and also obviously, she wasn't going to be comfortable trying to sleep on top of a black rock.

The small shoreline was littered with driftwood, mostly junker logs which had either been discarded by the logging companies or had broken free of booms being towed behind powerful tugs. It was easy to tell the junker logs from the natural ones—the junkers had chain-sawed ends. She supposed there was nothing anybody could do if a log managed to pop out of a boom load, but the discards angered and puzzled her. Anger because it would have been easier and cheaper to leave the tree standing if the trunk was twisted or otherwise deformed, and puzzlement because she had never been able to understand how people's minds worked or what could have happened to make them accept some things. Somehow the mentality which would clear-cut miles of vibrant forest, then leave masses of wood lying on the ground or rejected and dumped into the sea at the log sort grounds was the same as that which would inspire food fights. Fifteen million children under the age of ten starving to death every year, and in the name of harmless fun, people throw food at each other's laughing faces?

Meanwhile, some medical association or university or other statistics hound had done a study showing that more than 50 percent of North Americans were morbidly obese, and that another 30 percent or so were overweight, and another few percent were anorexic or bulimic, leaving less than one-eighth of the population in the vicinity of a normal, healthy weight.

Maybe you have to have had food rationed and doled out to you before you see it as something wonderful. Maybe you have to have been downright hungry before you see food as the gift of survival. Maybe if you've always had too much, you would benefit by having an experience of not enough. Or maybe you just needed a boot up the arse.

The boulders were huge, and grouped together in a near-perfect circle, with a wide crack on the side away from the sea. Cassidy knew she wasn't going to find any better place than this. She was protected from the wind no matter what direction it blew, and she would be comfortable as long as it didn't rain. She went back for her few things and brought them to the shelter, put them inside, then started looking for something to lay across the top. She dragged branches and small bits of log, some of them so thoroughly abraded by rocks and sand they had been flattened to thick planks. She worked until her arms ached and the tendons and muscles in her hands hurt. She had blisters on her palms and two nasty slivers dug into her fingers, but by the time the sun began to drop and the sky turned to a marvel of colour, Cassidy had her shelter. It was easy then to seek out small bits of summer-dry driftwood, feather-light cedar and bigger chunks of three-inch-thick fir bark.

She used sun-dried seaweed in place of paper, actually got it burning, then put bits of dry twig on it and, when that caught, bigger bits of cedar. And when she had the heartcore of a small fire, she dared to put several chunks of beach wood on it. The smoke rose almost straight up and drifted out the cracks of the covering that was supposed to be a roof.

Her jeans were still damp but her other things were dry. She pulled them on gratefully and sat in the warmth of the fire. The light was fading, but here, in this circular snuggy, she was comfortable, and the flying biters were kept at bay by the smoke. She leaned against a rock and stared at the flames, but her eyelids grew heavier and heavier, and she allowed herself to slide down to the sand, lying on her side with her head on her own arm.

When she wakened the fire was nearly out, only a few stubborn coals glowing in the dark. She added small bits of dry wood and sighed with relief when they started to burn. Her legs were cold and she ached from neck to Achilles tendon. She thought regretfully of the vanished egg salad sandwiches, then realized she wasn't actually hungry after all, just having a bout of scarcity mentality.

She poured coffee into the black plastic cup-lid of her stainless steel thermos, lit a cigarette and sat with her back against the rock. By now someone must have reported the Zodiac missing. Dawn would see the Coast Guard and probably the Air Force out looking for it. She would be able to build a fire on the beach and put damp seaweed on it so the smoke would be thick and easily seen. In the summertime you could hardly make it through a newscast without some item about boaters or fishers plucked safely from certain death. You hardly ever heard of people just vanishing forever. And she had never heard of someone who had survived a violent dunking, managed to set herself up in a little rock womb, and then perished for lack of egg salad sandwiches. Of course they'd find her. And if they didn't, well, there were sure to be oysters or at least mussels clinging to these rocks. She wasn't sure there was any water, however. And she knew nobody lived long without water.

She almost panicked then. It was one thing to accept the possibility of being stranded for an indefinite period of time on what was probably the top of a mountain sticking up out of the sea, and quite another to think of perishing of thirst. From everything she'd seen in movies and on TV, it was an awful death, slow and painful. Well, before she'd check out that way she'd leap into the ocean and drown quickly.

The firelight flickered on the rocks and for the first time Cassidy noticed faint hints of what seemed to be graven patterns. Of course not, they couldn't be, it must be nothing more than the action of the high waves of neap tide. She had seen gorgeous patterns carved into sandstone and rocks by wind and tide, but never anything quite as regular as these. They looked for all the world like spirals, or interlocking chains, or even braiding.

Intrigued, Cassidy held her cigarette and thermos lid in one hand and bent forward for a better look. The roof of her womblike home was too low for her to stand, and hunkered over she couldn't get a very good look, her body was blocking the faint firelight. She knelt and leaned forward, cigarette smoke wreathing faintly in front of her, rising past the designs toward the roof. With her free hand she traced the whorls. She didn't feel anything flaky or dry or the least bit suggestive of lichen or moss, but there must have been something like that there, and her gentle touch must have dislodged it, because when she withdrew her hand, the places she had touched were more obvious, more noticeable. Maybe there was moisture on the rockface and when she touched it, it was like drawing on a steamy window. Now she could see that the pattern was definitely one of spirals, some of them joined by braids, or what looked like a cable stitch. Fascinated, she reached out again and deliberately retraced the pattern. It showed even more clearly, as if her finger could engrave the rock, scribe lines and curves in living stone.

Cassidy chose an area with no hint of design, and carefully, wetting her finger in the cooling coffee, she drew a picture of the Zodiac, tipping, with figures tumbling into the waves. She expected her picture to last only a few seconds and then, as the coffee dried, to vanish forever. But the pattern did not disappear. She stared at it, knowing what she was looking at had to be a mirage. Anything else was impossible. Mirage or not, there it was, and she watched as her hand reached forward as if it had a mind of its own and drew a second picture, one lone figure separated from the Zodiac and the other figures. She was dimly surprised at how well she could draw. She had never been particularly good at drawing, and as a child she had been bored almost to nausea by the wretched chore of colouring pictures. People had kept giving her these damn jumbo colouring books and expecting her to colour the figures with her collection of wax crayons. Just the thought of staying inside the lines of a meaningless picture someone else had drawn had been enough to make her impatient. "Oh, look," they would say with false cheer, "here's a lovely little piglet with a happy smile on his face. What colour are you going to use for him?" She had wished for a crayon which worked like an eraser so she could drag it over the heavy black lines, make them invisible and leave the page blank so it could be used for something worthwhile. Like writing her own story. Or drawing her own picture. But no, the crayons came in an assortment of shades and tones of just about any colour a person could think of, and nobody seemed to believe a child might want to draw her own pictures. It was too important to force her to learn how to colour in pictures other people had drawn. "Not much co-ordination," they decided. "Seems like she can't stay inside the lines." None of them entertained the idea that she hadn't tried, that she didn't want to, that she had deliberately scribbled a hasty mess to shut them up for a while.

She drew a third picture, the lone figure sitting cross-legged, staring out at nothing. Then, because the third picture seemed inadequate or unfinished, and somehow not the least bit true, she drew a second figure. Now it seemed complete. She traced her little history scenes over and over, graving the designs deeper, her cigarette dead, her coffee cold.

In her old life, she would have dumped the cold coffee, but she thought of the lack of water and poured it back into the thermos instead, just in case this wasn't a dream after all. So many strange things had happened, her overloaded and near-numb brain did not register the fact that despite the fact she had enjoyed two cups of coffee, her four-cup thermos was still almost full. Nor did she register the fact that even though she had filled the thermos hours or days ago, and poured cold coffee back in, the coffee was still hot.

She was suddenly more tired than she had ever been in her life. It was like filling a brown paper bag with water: for a brief period, the bag accomplishes the impossible and holds the liquid. Then, suddenly, the bottom is gone and the water drops to the ground with a splat, and there you are holding some soggy paper. Just like that, her wakefulness was gone. *Whump.* She slumped to the sandy ground and closed her eyes.

When she wakened, sunlight came in through the door opening, slanting into the cracks of her whapped-together roof. Cassidy sat up and the first thing she saw was the markings on the rock—sworls, spirals, cable stitch patterns and her own pictures. When she reached out to touch them she could feel how deeply they were cut into the rock. Her hand was only slightly dirty, her fingertips calloused, and just above her wrist, a third of the way to her elbow, was a tattoo-like design of spirals joined by what looked like squared-off chain links. It occurred to her that they were supposed to signify the eternal maze of recurrent lives.

She left her little hoochie and went outside. The sun was barely above the rim of the sea, the eastern sky stained and streaked morning red, with huge feather-pattern clouds of white. Out on the sea a junker log was floating and on it were four cormorants, sitting side-by-each. Gulls bobbed on the water and a seal stared at her, round-eyed.

She walked slowly along the rock and sand beach until she found a colony of oysters clinging to rocks just under the waterline. She had to use a stone to bang some of the shells loose, but in very little time she had eight of them which she took back to the hoochie. She had to relight her fire and she scolded herself for letting it go out in the first place, when she could easily have added fuel while she was busy getting callouses on her fingers from the surface of the rock. When the fire was established and burning steadily, she placed the oysters, shell and all, on rocks near the heat. Almost immediately the seawater inside began to hiss and bubble, small wisps of steam issuing from the crack where the two plates of shell met.

Cassidy lit a cigarette and poured a cup of hot coffee from her three-quarters-full thermos. She supposed she ought to feel wretched, ought to be almost hysterical, frantic with the need to be rescued. Instead, she felt at peace. She knew her feelings were inappropriate and she didn't care. There were no feeling-police on this boulder with her, no emotion-cops, no thought-controllers. She hoped her daughters and granddaughters would have sense enough not to get their shirts in a knot once they found out she was, as they say, missing. She didn't feel missing, even though others might think she was. She wished she could send them a telegram: Not to worry, all is well, love Mom. She realized the telegram hadn't said Wish you were here. Well, you don't tell lies at so much per word! She didn't wish they were here. Right now she didn't even wish that she was there. Not to worry, all is well. And in a way, all was very well. The oysters were opening as they cooked, the coffee was delicious, the cigarette possibly the most satisfying of her long career as a lung-punisher, and her wall engravings were beautiful. What more did she need?

Michael had hated Cassidy's coffee and cigarettes routine in the morning. He wanted a pot of tea. It didn't satisfy him that Cassidy would gladly make him his tea, poach two eggs, make toast, set the table and always remember to put out the small jar of Scottish marmalade. He wanted her to eat breakfast and drink tea, too. When she made coffee for herself he would sniff contemptuously and, every morning for thirty-plus years, say, "I don't know how you can stand to swallow that swill." If she had lit a cigarette at that moment, he would have pitched his breakfast in her face. Rather than wear the eggs she had so carefully poached, Cassidy took her coffee with her and went out on the sundeck to drink it. Spring, summer, autumn or winter, there she was on the sundeck, drinking Columbian and enjoying her first Player's filter. She smoked most of her cigarettes outside, Michael complained so much about the smell of them. The smell of his after-dinner cigar didn't bother him, but that, like so much else, was different.

She ate her oysters slowly, feeling she had never tasted anything so good even though she had eaten at some of the most classy restaurants. Michael wouldn't have been caught dead in a diner or greasy spoon. She had eaten oysters done with elegant sauces, drenched in white wine, smothered in out-of-season fresh spinach, and coddled in extravagant concoctions of chefs' artistry, and not one of those dinners had come close to this one. Cassidy supposed it helped to be so hungry your hands shook.

And yet, as hungry as she had been when she started, she couldn't finish all the oysters she had prepared. She didn't want to waste anything—there had to be a limit to how many of them could grow on this chuck-surrounded mountaintop. She put them near the graven wall, to save for later.

Her hands and forearms were sticky with oyster juice and her mouth was smeared. It didn't matter how she looked, but she had such a total terror of wasps she went outside to wash in the sea. She stripped off her clothes and carefully washed the fire soot and oyster drippings from them, then lay them on the rocks to dry. She'd know better from now on, she'd make sure she didn't spill anything on them. Wasps would go at anything that smelled the least little bit like something they could eat, and they were prepared to eat anything. Naked, she stepped into the water. It was bitterly cold and she started shivering almost immediately. But it was very important to be clean. She ought to have done this before she ate. A person should respect herself, respect her food. Cassidy wondered where that thought had come from. Probably from all those years of being told to wash her hands before coming to the table.

When she came from the water she was still shivering and felt chilled to the bone. She lay on the flat-topped smooth black stone and let the sun warm her. She fell asleep even though she hadn't intended to, and wakened only when thirst and an urgent need to pee forced her awake. She didn't want to pee near her hoochie, she should have sought out a place before now, somewhere distant enough neither sight nor smell would offend.

And what an odd word to choose. Offend. Offend who? Well, herself, of course, but still, a strange choice.

She found her place, and with a piece of beach stick and a hunk of rock, she dug a pit. No sooner was it dug than she realized she had more to do than just piddle in it. She hoped wasps weren't so voracious they would arrive before she had time to use a handful of moss, then cover up her leavings. Wouldn't that be just too much, to be stung on the arse by a wasp while stranded on a mountaintop in the middle of nowhere.

She spent the day hauling firewood, stacking most of it near her hoochie and using some of it to build a teepee-shaped pile. This she intended to set alight at the first hint of the sound of a motor. She didn't care if it was a plane, heli-copter, freighter, fish boat or yacht, any motor would do.

She checked her clothes often, and when they were again bone dry she took them into the hoochie. The oysters she had left for later were gone. The shells were there, but the meat was missing. She suspected wasps, except she didn't hear them droning and hadn't really seen one, except in her own fears. Puzzled, she tended her fire, then went outside and down the beach to hammer a few more oysters off the rocks. Then she went back to scanning the skies, listening for the sound of search and rescue aircraft.

She didn't hear the faintest hint, and when the sun set and the heat faded, she went back into the hoochie. The oysters she had picked were gone, their empty shells neatly lined up beside the others, in front of the graven wall. It was too much to think about. When she tried, her mind clicked off like a wall switch. Still naked, she went again to the oyster bed and once more she rapped off enough for a meal. This time she put them around the fire to bake and kept a close watch on them while she pulled on her underpants, jeans and shirt.

The same kind of oysters, picked from the same bed, cooked in the same way around the fire, and they tasted different than the last ones. Better. Much better. She felt as if she could have eaten twice as many, and yet again she was full. Was that how people wound up getting so heavy they could hardly heave themselves up out of a chair? Did food always taste so good to them they ate more, wanting the taste even when they knew their stomachs were full? Did they just keep cramming it down, need it or not, because it tasted so good?

She treated herself to a cup of coffee and a cigarette, and sat, her back against a rock, looking across the glow of the bed of coals at the graven wall. She let her eyes follow the patterns, over and over again until she didn't need to see the wall, or see the carvings, she could close her eyes and see them. Not just imagine them, *see* them.

And when she opened her eyes again, the bed of coals was dim, she had to find small pieces of dry wood and feed them in carefully, blowing on them. She didn't feel as if she had been asleep, but she must have sat for a long time, inwardly seeing the patterns and designs carved into the rocks.

And she knew what they were. Knew why the oysters had disappeared. Knew so much, and none of it would have "made sense" to the ones she had been told all her life were normal people. She knew, and accepted, and more.

Cassidy very carefully arranged the empty shells, then into one of them she poured some of her cherished coffee. She could see the steam rising toward the patterns, could smell the coffee, and it had never seemed more inviting. She wanted to drink it herself, but didn't. She consciously and willingly gave it. Then lit a cigarette and carefully placed it in a second shell. Maybe the egg salad sandwiches had just up and vanished with no thought or consciousness on her part, but this much, at least, she could give.

She knew before she looked that the design on her arm was clearer now, knew too it was larger, more intricate. And knew she was not intended to trace copies of these designs on the rocks. She was to use her finger, her own flesh, to write her own story, here and now, not expecting anyone but herself to read it, free from any threat of editing or criticism, for purposes she might not understand but could intuit deeply, and she knew she had no chance at all to truly survive, unless she did.

– VII –

They were partying again. He was home from fishing with money falling from every pocket, and the last thing that would occur to him, or to her, was to put some of it into the bank. No, hell no, he'd been gone almost three months, he'd worked hard for it, damn hard, and what was it for anyway but to spend. Both she and Tim had new clothes, new shoes, even radios for their bedrooms and new quilts for their beds. Tim had a brand new shiny black three-speed bicycle, Cassidy's was bright fire-engine red. It was hard for them to feel they were wasting money when they were spending so much of it on her and Tim.

And easy to think of it as wasted, later on when it was gone. No more steak dinners, but meal after meal of rice and fish, fish and rice, rice with fish, fish with rice, fish *in* rice and, for a change, mashed potato mixed with fish and made into little cakes, then fried until brown and crispy. When things got really lean she would go out in the little rowboat, jig some rock cod, bring them home and fillet them, then slice potato and layer it with the fish. She would let it stand for a couple of hours, so that when she cooked it up, both the fish and the potato tasted like fish. A person got tired of the taste of spuds a lot quicker than she got tired of the taste of rock cod.

But for a while it was steak, or pork chops, sometimes roast, with potatoes and vegetables cooked all around it. Cassidy did the cooking, because Tina was always too busy partying. "Only way to be sure to save my marriage," she maundered, often. "He's going to go out beering, and if I don't go with him, someone else will." It was an easy excuse. Plenty of times when he was out on the chuck, days or weeks gone, Tina would start partying again with someone else because, she always said, trying to make it sound like a joke, anybody who drinks alone has a problem.

For a while it looked as if Cassidy was going to have to cook supper for the whole mad pack of them, but someone got a bright idea, and they phoned for two cabs and went off in them, yahooing and hoorawing and having a wonderful time. They'd been playing poker and there was money on the table, so Cassidy took it. She didn't count it, she just stuffed it in her jeans pocket. Tim just nodded when he saw her do it. He knew they'd probably need it before long. Save enough crumbs from the table and sooner or later you'll have enough for a loaf. Or at least a pound or two of hamburger to break the monotony of rice and fish.

The house looked as if a herd of elephants had stampeded through it. While the spuds were cooking, Cassidy and Tim did what they could to tidy up the worst of the mess. Tim took the empty beer bottles outside, to the stack he had in the far corner of the woodshed. First chance he got he would take them to the bottle depot, turn them in for money, then give at least some of the money to Cassidy. But never all of it. Tim had a big broad streak of West Coast fisherman in him, too, and when he had money in his pocket, everybody had money. That's why Cassidy tried to keep the crumbs in her possession.

She cooked fresh corn and they ate it doused with margarine and sprinkled with black pepper. That and the spuds, touched with the juice from the frying pan where she'd cooked the steaks, made a fine supper. They packed it all away, then Cassidy did up the dishes, cleaned the kitchen, swept and washed the floor. Tim half-assedly tidied the living room, not doing much more than collecting and emptying the overflowing ashtrays.

He went out then, Cassidy had no idea where. There was no reason for him to tell her, no reason for her to be interested. He had his own group of friends and Cassidy didn't particularly like them. The girls laughed at anything the boys said and were always pulling out little pocket mirrors, looking in them, and either putting on or wiping off lipstick. When the boys said rude things or leered and patted them on the backside, they pretended to resist, flapping their hands ineffectually and saying things like Oh, you! You stop that, you hear. The boys seldom stopped and the girls seldom minded. They seemed to think of it as some kind of flattery. Cassidy would have liked to be able to convince herself the girls were all stupid, but the truth of it was they made her feel self-conscious. She couldn't behave the way they did and she knew it. What was worse, they knew it too. Sometimes she'd be walking down the street on her way to do the family shopping, and she'd pass a group of girls standing together like a flock of hens. She had said hello and been ignored so often she now walked past as if they weren't even there. But they were there, and no sooner was she past them than they giggled. Always. Cassidy was convinced they were laughing at her. She would have liked to whirl, to confront them, to tell them all off, but then they'd really have something to laugh about and the story would be all over town within hours.

She could have done homework, but she didn't. She lay on her bed, listened to her radio and thumbed through the detective magazines Tim shoplifted as fast as they came into the stores. The pictures were grainy and so badly focussed they might have been just about anything, you pretty well had to believe what they said in the captions. Unless it was something without people, like the bloodstained bed, or the open trunk of a car. Or police photos. Some of the men in the pictures looked the way you'd expect them to look, capable of slaughtering any number of people. Others looked like they worked in shoe stores or gas stations and you wouldn't think they'd even lose their temper, but they must have done, to be found guilty of such awful things.

Tim came home first, well past midnight, and he didn't even brush his teeth, let alone have a shower. She heard him come in the house, go to the bathroom, have a pee without flushing the toilet, then go to his bedroom. He probably wouldn't even undress, he'd just flop into his unmade bed. At least he slipped off his shoes. Sometimes the old man came home and got into bed, shoes and all. Of course he had to be well and truly packed to do that. And Tina had to be well and truly packed too, or she'd take them off for him.

Tina wasn't anybody's mother. There hadn't been a mother in the house for years. Cassidy could remember her, but only dimly. She could remember too when Mom had packed everybody's clothes into suitcases and boxes from the store, then called a cab and took boxes and children to the bus depot. They had a long ride on the bus, and then stayed for a few days with Auntie Joan while Mom found a house to rent. It was nice living there, with cousins just down the street and a sidewalk where they could chalk in the design and play hopscotch. But it all ended a week or so after fishing season closed. The old man showed up and it wasn't just roar and bluster, he meant business and let the world know it. Kicked in the door. Wrecked the kitchen. Beat Mom up so bad the neighbours called the cops. Before they arrived, the old fool dragged Cassidy and Tim out to the car where a couple of his buddies were waiting.

There had been a big go-round, and then the cops came to the house and took the old man away in the back of their car. At first it seemed as if he was going to go quietly, but when they closed the door on him, he slid across the back seat and tried to open the one on the other side. That's when he found out the only way to get in or out of the back seat was from the outside. There was a metal mesh grill between the back seat and the front. He roared with frustration, then demonstrated to the police and the neighbours just what a mesatchie he could be. He lay on his back and kicked his legs at the windows until the cops got mad, opened the door, managed to grab onto him and put handcuffs on his wrists, then tied his ankles together and ran a rope up to the cuffs. Every time he tried to kick he jerked himself into a backward arch.

Cassidy and Tim went to stay with Auntie Joan. It was a wonderful two weeks. There were cousins to play with, and if they went to bed much earlier than they were accustomed, nobody yelled at them to turn off the goddamn light and stop the noise, they were allowed to chatter (quietly) and giggle (quietly) until Auntie Joan came to the door and told them they only had another few minutes until lights out. When she came back, she didn't just flip the switch, either, she went from one to the other for a good long cuddle and some smooches and only when each of them was feeling very special and very loved did she leave, and turn out the light as she went. There was blackberry pie for dessert, as long as they picked the berries, and applesauce, if they picked the transparents and helped peel them.

But then the old man was at Auntie Joan's and they knew the holiday was over. He didn't rant and rave right there. He even managed to be polite, and stay for supper, and compliment Mom's sister on her cooking and baking. Well, he had to be polite and behave like a human person, because Uncle Gillam was at home for fire season, and he was at least twice the size and three times the strength of the old man.

Cassidy was never sure what had been said in court, or out of it for that matter, but the old man got custody. As close to a clue as she ever got was his repeated gloating that he made enough money he could convince the judge she and Tim would be better off with him than with Mom, who was working as a waitress. When Mom's lawyer tried to counter by pointing out the old man was gone to the fishing grounds for months every year, the old man said that was no different than shift work, except he would be able to hire someone to live in full time to care for them.

And each time he bragged about it he would wind up saying, "Money talks, bullshit walks," and his cronies would laugh and nod and agree with him. They were supposed to be able to see Mom every second weekend and spend half their school holidays with her, but she lived too far away for the weekends and somehow the other didn't happen. When she got her holidays she would come down to stay with Aunt Joan and they'd see her then, but she cried so much each time that it wasn't much fun and after a while even that stopped.

Tina started off as the housekeeper. The old man ran an ad in the paper and several different women showed up, but

Tina was the one he chose. Of course. She could cook, but nothing fancy, and she could bake, but not very well. What she seemed to do best was laugh and toss her hair. And pop the buttons on her shirts. With the old man off fishing things were pretty flat, they might as well have been living in a hotel—one that didn't bother with chambermaids, because she never even told them to tidy their rooms, let alone make a move to do it herself. She did laundry when the basket was so full nothing else would go into it, the sink was usually at least half full of dishes, and the one place she and the kids agreed, the only place, really, was that she would yell at them to get the hell out of the house and go play somewhere, and they were eager to do exactly that.

School let out and Cassidy was passed from grade two to three while Tim went from grade one to grade two. Tina didn't even look at their report cards when they came home with them. But Aunt Joan asked if they could go stay with her for part of the summer and Tina said sure, why not, do 'em good, and there they got some pats on the back for having done well. Mom came to see them, and she cried, and sometimes at night Cassidy would hear her talking to Aunt Joan about how it wasn't fair.

"There are cafes and restaurants here," Aunt Joan said every time. "You could move back, get a job, be close enough to them to see them often. Even *he* isn't stupid enough to say no to the idea of you having them all summer."

"You don't know him! If I was anywhere near he'd hound me half to distraction. It would be banging on the door at night, it would be rocks through the window, it would be him out howling and yelling in the moonlight. You just don't know."

Cassidy didn't know, either. Maybe it would have been

like that, maybe not. In any event Mom was gone a couple of weeks later, back to her job and her new life, the one she said was dull, uninteresting and nothing but hard work and hot tears. Aunt Joan sniffed when Mom said that.

Tina made no move at all to bring them home so they stayed, happy as clams in deep water, until just before school started. They might have gone back to school in last year's clothes except Aunt Joan had words with Tina.

"I happen to know that the whole time they've been at my place you've still been paid for looking after them, and you've had the grocery money in your hand as well! So just unearth some of it and give it to me. I'm getting them some new clothes."

"Who do you think you are, anyway! I'm the one in charge here."

"You're the one will be in jail for fraud in about half an hour if you don't mind your pees and queues, Miss Flip! There's a welfare department in town and it won't take me but a few minutes to get there. And the police station is even closer than that."

So off they went, first to the bank where Tina took out some money, and then down to the stores. Aunt Joan wasn't one for browns and dark blues, either.

The old man came home and wasn't back a week when Tina went from "housekeeper" to "housekeeper, so to speak." That meant she moved from the spare room into the old man's room, and put her clothes in his closet and her shoes under his bed. She seemed to think the move entitled her to go from being Tina to being Mom, but it didn't happen. Not then nor at any other time.

"All I do for you," she would whine, usually when she was half packed and getting ready to gear herself up to go out and

find a party, "and what do I get by way of thank you? Bugger
nothing, is what I get from you two ungrateful mutts."

At first they just listened to it, the resentful words dropping on them like hot coals, hurting them, making them feel
helpless, but eventually Cassidy learned to give as good as
she got. "Do for us? Just what is it you do for us, Tina? You're
well paid as near as I can tell. Not many people get a chance
to sit on their fat asses and still have money to spend!"

"You'd be in an orphanage if it wasn't for me!"

"We'd be with Aunt Joan and Uncle Gillam if it wasn't for
you, you mean!"

At night she would lie awake, seething with resentment,
wishing things were different, spinning great fantasies about
how she and Tim would manage to intercept some money
somehow, maybe forge Tina's name and get the money from
the bank or maybe . . . something . . . and then they'd take
the bus and live with Mom. And wouldn't everything be
wonderful!

Except the visits weren't happening after the summer she
went from grade five to grade six. Mom had come down, but
she only stayed a week, and she didn't hold onto them and
cry about how much she missed them. She seemed happy
enough to see them, but happy the way a person is when they
see, say, a niece or nephew. Something was gone. Worn out
or broken or lost, or tossed in the trash. And at night, when
Mom sat at the table with tea and blackberry tarts and talked
to Aunt Joan, it wasn't about how unfair things were, or how
she was working toward some changes that would allow
them to live with her. All she could talk about was some guy
named Sam, and how happy he was about the coming baby,
and how she was going to use the rest of her holiday to move
from the auto court to this little house, with a yard and even

a bit of a garden space cleared in the backyard. There was a big two-car garage, too, and Sam was going to be able to have his own little after-hours repair shop, not just work for someone else for the rest of his life but get a start on what would eventually be his own business.

Cassidy thought the coming baby was Sam's baby and it wasn't until well past Easter she realized it was Mom's baby, too, and she and Tim had been replaced. When she said as much, Aunt Joan tried to smooth it out.

"No, dear, never!" she protested. "You will always be your mommy's girl, and Tim will always be your mommy's firstborn son, it's only different in that she's given you a little baby brother now."

"What kind of a brother is it if you've never even seen it?"

"Oh, but look at these pictures! Isn't he just the sweetest little brother a girl could have? And he looks *just* like you did when you were wee."

Except he didn't. She knew, because everybody said so often enough, that both she and Tim took after their father. And if Sam was this baby's father it made no sense at all that he and Cassidy would resemble each other.

And that summer Mom didn't make it down at all. The baby, she said, was too young to travel easily. As if anyone expected a baby to have to pack his stuff and do the driving! All a baby had to do was be a baby, and sleep and suck a bottle and puke and get carried around and get his diaper changed. And he could do that on the bus as easily as in a house.

Tina gloated. Not with words, but with the way she behaved. She had it by the horns, now. Absolutely no fear of the old man cleaning up his act and talking Mom into coming back home. Not just a new man in the picture but a baby too.

Tina was drinking more and more all the time. Not just at home, by herself, but other places too. And when the old man was off fishing, Tina was off beering. Cassidy was twelve going on thirteen now, and could do for herself and Tim just fine. And a good job, too, because otherwise they might have gone hungry.

"Fine, then, be that way," she would say, "but if you don't chop some kindling and fill the wood box, just see if I'm going to cook supper."

"Did God die and make you the boss?" Tim would yell. "When did *you* become my mother, anyway?"

"I don't care one way or the other, little boy. I can cook supper for myself and *you* can burn something and try to eat it. If you don't help me, why should I do anything for you?"

He made noises but he did his chores. And when they had eaten, she washed dishes and he dried them. His room looked like a combination logging camp, motorcycle repair shop and junkyard, but when Cassidy filled the machine and started sorting the wash, he helped.

The washing machine had probably been on the ark, but at least it got things cleaner than they had been when they went in. They figured out for themselves that if they cut a piece from an old inner tube and fitted it around the metal screw-tipped shaft of the agitator post they could get the metal paddle to not only sit there but stay there, instead of wobbling or not moving at all. They couldn't fix the pump that was supposed to drain the water, but Tim moved the whole riggin's onto the back porch so they could just drop the drain hose over the edge and empty the drum. And it was Tim found an adapter end so they could attach the garden hose to the hot water tap in the kitchen and fill the machine that way.

"That's using the old bean," the old man said when he saw the buckshee riggin's. "Whose idea was this?"

"Tim figured it out." Cassidy knew she sounded as if she was bragging, and maybe she was. After all, Tim was her brother. "He's pretty smart, huh?"

"Not bad, not bad at all," and from the old man that was praise.

Of course, it didn't mean he treated Tim any better than he ever had. He must have had the idea his son would be born with the strength and savvy of an adult male, because some of the tasks he set were impossible for a boy. And when Tim couldn't do them, the old man would haul off his belt and whale at him until Cassidy wanted to scream and run for the cops. She found a good way to put a stop to some of it, though. Once when Tim was on the floor, not even able to cry, and the old man was shellacking him, whap, whap, whap, whap, regularly, monotonously, whap, whap, whap, all of a sudden, no warning at all, Cassidy was puking.

"Jesus Christ almighty!" the old man roared.

"*Stop it!*" she screeched hysterically, between belly-clenching cramps. "*Stop it*, you're *killing* him!"

"You stupid bitch. Look at the mess. You get busy and clean it up!" and he let her have several whaps with the belt across her back and shoulders. Then he stood yelling, his face so red it was almost purple, his eyes bugged wide, but at least he was yelling at her and not pounding on poor Tim.

He and Tina stormed out of the house before the floor was cleaned up, and Cassidy got Tim into bed. He looked awful. So awful she was terrified, and ran down to the corner store to use the phone. The old man wouldn't have a phone in the house, he'd got the idea somewhere that there were what he called "emanations" from it that made people sick.

Aunt Joan and Uncle Gillam came right away. Aunt Joan started to cry, but Uncle Gillam just picked Tim up and walked out to the car with him. They all got in the car and took Tim to the hospital.

She hated the way everyone looked at her, as if somehow she herself was to blame for what the old man was, what he did. As if she had chosen to be born into such a screwball mess. She was just about ready to open her mouth and convince them of their already-held opinion when the doctor said they had to take Tim to the operating room because he was bleeding inside, and that seemed so awful there wasn't any room left for her own resentment about the looks on people's faces.

They wheeled the stretcher into the elevator and when the doors closed, Aunt Joan started to cry again. Uncle Gillam didn't cry. He drove them both back to the house and told Aunt Joan to start packing some of Cassidy's stuff, he'd be back soon.

Cassidy wished she could have gone with him, just to see it. But she heard about it enough that it was almost as good as seeing it. The old man and Tina were sitting at a round-topped table in the Occidental Hotel when Uncle Gillam walked in and looked around. He saw them before they saw him. In fact they didn't see him at all until he had the old man out of his chair and up in the air. Uncle Gillam carried the old man that way, out of the bar, onto the street, then down the alley. When he let him down, he let him all the way down, and threw him into the wall of the Occie. "There, you mean-minded fish-stinking bastard of a netminder," he roared. "You threw the wee boy into the wall, and now you know what that feels like!" And to be sure the old man did, Uncle Gillam picked him up again and gave him another toss into the wall.

Then he took off his belt and started whaling away, roaring, "Tit for tat you fuckin' jackass bastard!" Each time the old man tried to stand up to ward off the belt, Uncle Gillam gave him a kick or a punch and hammered him back down again. The one poor deluded soul who tried to put a stop to it got bounced on his ass so hard they all said he was two inches shorter when he stood up again.

And the cops just stood in the alley, watching. No way they were going to take on Gillam. When it was over, and the old man was in even worse shape than Tim had been, they took him and Gillam to the station. Gillam went quietly, hoisting the old man under his arm and carrying him to the paddy wagon. He told the what and the why of it. One of the cops went up to the hospital to verify the story and came back ashen-faced with fury and disgust.

They had the old man checked over but when the doctor said there were no internal injuries and nothing broken, they took him back down to the pokey and tossed him in a cell. Gillam was asked to not go overboard like that again, please, and allowed to leave without any charges being laid.

"It's up to him," they decided. "If he wants to lay charges, well, the judge will hear them, but we aren't laying any."

"If he tries to lay charges," Gillam grinned, "he'll be so goddamn sorry none of us will believe it."

"Oh, I believe it," one of the cops said, and he laughed.

And yet, two weeks later, the old man had a court order in his hand and Tim and Cassidy had to go back home. Well, not Tim, not right away, he was still in the hospital with a scar on his belly that looked as if they'd opened him up and then put in a zipper or a railway track.

But the insane beatings stopped. Which didn't mean the regular ones stopped, just the insane ones. There were still sudden unexplained slaps to the side of the head, quick boots to the backside, or brutal shoves that sent each, either or both of them across the room, cringing and trying to protect their heads and faces. And by now Cassidy had to try to protect her growing breasts as well.

Tina laughed. "Just shows to go ya!" she would cackle. "Now you know! Take a telling!" and other stupid things, but Tina was increasingly stupid.

"Pickled your damn brain, haven't you," Cassidy screeched, but only when the old man was off fishing. "Keep it up you'll be too stupid to find your own arse to wipe it."

"Hell, she doesn't wipe it now," Tim cracked. "She doesn't have to. She opens her mouth and the shit runs out from there."

"You'll be sorry when your father gets home." Tina's big weapon, but it didn't have the effect it once had.

"You're the one'll be sorry if you don't shape up. He'll dump you and get one that can at least walk across the room without falling on her face."

More than once Tim had to tackle Tina and hold her down while she raved and yelled about how the walls were falling down, or splitting open and spewing spiders. "Are you blind?" she screamed. "Jesus, don't you *see* them?" Several times they struggled to get her to her bed, then tied her down, but she made so much noise they eventually let her up and she lurched out of the house cursing.

The old man didn't pay any attention to what they told him about it but he heard what his buddies said, and though he didn't give her the boot, he did make some changes in the way things got handled.

"So, can you be trusted?" he said sternly to Cassidy. "If I change the bank account so you can cash the cheques and

all, can you make sure the electric is paid and there's groceries and such?"

"I can do that," Cassidy told him firmly, "and do it a lot
better than she ever did."

"Don't get lippy, bitch." But he wasn't really mad at her,
and they both knew it. "Show some respect."

"For her?" Cassidy snorted.

She wasn't yet fourteen by the time she was running the
house. Tina still got what she called her wages, so she still had
plenty of money for the booze with which she was killing herself, but she didn't have access to anything else and she
resented it totally.

Without saying a word to anyone, Cassidy opened an
account in her own name at the Bank of Montreal and began
snitching from the household funds, putting them in what she
thought of as Going Away Money. The old man didn't notice,
he didn't even suspect. Cassidy figured if Tina was being paid
enough to send her around the bend, supposedly for being
housekeeper, cook and general factotum, then Cassidy, who
was actually doing all that as well as babysitting Tina half the
time, was entitled to pay as well.

Tim was twelve and Cassidy almost fourteen when
changes began which Cassidy knew were previews of the
near future. The day school let out, Tim left to go fishing. Not
with the old man—they both knew what a mess that would
be, probably winding up with one or the other or both of
them being food for crabs. Tim headed out with Einarr
Gunnarson on his two-man troller.

Einarr didn't talk much but he nodded a lot, as if he
agreed with everything a person said and thought the world
was as good a place as it could be, all things considered. He
had never married although it was rumoured he had three

kids by two different women on the reserve. When Einarr got to drinking he became even quieter than usual, if that was possible, and he smiled more broadly. He was thought of as one of the most reliable fishers on the coast, and if he didn't bring in as much as some of the bigger boats, there wasn't a boat the size of his did as well. And he didn't mind at all going out with someone who knew next best thing to nothing and teaching them. More than one good fisher had started out working for and eventually with Einarr. Cassidy knew Tim was lucky, and knew Einarr wasn't taking Tim with him because he felt any special obligation to the old man. Einarr had no use for him at all.

She also knew, as if it had been passed as law, that Tim would come back from fishing and return to school this time and several times more, because you had to go to school until you finished grade eight or turned fifteen, whichever came first. But Tim wasn't going to finish high school, or graduate, or go on to trades training or university and wind up wearing a suit to work. Their kind of people didn't do things like that.

She didn't talk it over with the old man, or with Tina. What business was it of theirs, and why bother? Tim hadn't asked permission to get his job, and the old man was already gone anyway. As for Tina, you couldn't talk sense with her most of the time, but even if she'd been sober and sane it had nothing to do with her. Cassidy just pulled some money out of her Going Away fund and outfitted Tim for the summer. He was Going Away, after all. And to Go Away, and Go properly, there were things he would need.

"Jeez, Cass, this is great," but he didn't hug her, he didn't kiss her, he didn't even shake her hand. Those too were things their kind of people didn't do.

She stood on the weather-worn dock and waved as the boat pulled away. Both Tim and Einarr waved briefly, and then, too fast for Cassidy, they were gone.

That left her alone with Tina. And Cassidy had no intention of being alone with Tina. She went back to the house, packed some things, walked to town and caught the bus to Aunt Joan's place.

It was her last summer of real fun. She got a part-time some-time job, but it didn't interfere with the truly important things in life—swimming, picking berries for pie, harvesting fruit, helping with the canning and jam-making and preserving.

Mom came down with her three new kids, but Sam couldn't make it because there was just too much work at the auto repair shop. Freddie, Peter and Janet were nice little kids, and they were ready to fall fully and totally in love with their big sister. Cassidy pushed them on the big swing in the backyard, she walked the beach with them and showed them the small crabs which lived under the rocks, she taught them about the dime-sized holes in the sand and how, if they dug fast enough, they could haul out horse clams. Everyone said how nice it was that she was so fond of her little brothers and sister, and Cassidy felt like a total hypocrite because she didn't give two hoots in hell one way or the other. People might call them her brothers and sister, but nobody had asked her!

"I'm so proud of you," Mom said.

Cassidy was astonished. "Me?"

"Yes, you. You're so . . . reliable, so . . . steady," and she looked as if she expected Cassidy to say something, but all Cassidy could do was shake her head quickly and turn away, mute.

The part-time some-time job was hard, heavy work, but satisfying. Aunt Joan would help her pack a lunch before bedtime, and then, when her alarm went off, Cassidy would be out of bed and into her jeans and long-sleeved shirt as quickly and quietly as possible, so she wouldn't waken the cousins who were still sleeping. They envied her the job but were a couple of years away from being able to get their own.

She washed her face and brushed her hair, tying it back and tucking it under the faded red ball cap. Then, with her lunch and some fruit in a bag in the carrier of the bike, she pedalled to the gas station on the highway. They had a bicycle stand there, and she could leave her borrowed CCM without worrying someone would swipe it. She stood with the others, waiting for the flat-decked truck, and when it arrived they climbed on and were bounced and jiggled to the next field.

Most of the farmers were still doing hay the hard way. Only a few of the bigger, richer farms had balers. Cassidy spent the day with a three-tined fork, lifting the cured hay from the windrows and putting it on the wagon. When the pile on the wagon was too high for them, a couple of the guys climbed up, tramped the hay, then stood with forks to take the hay from Cassidy and the others and lift it to the stack. When one wagon was full, off it went and another took its place. Sometimes the wagons were drawn by trucks or tractors, but often the replacement wagon was pulled by horses.

She wore out four pair of leather gloves that summer, and the palms of her hands and fingers were slick and shiny with callous. "Farm hands," they joked. "This is what they mean by farm hands. We could steal the bank blind and they'd never even get fingerprints, they're all wore off."

Too soon it was time to go back to town. Not back

"home." Back to town, to the rented house where Tina was shambling and shaking, the old man was roaring and hollering, and Tim was waiting for the day he finished grade eight. "If I work at it," he told her solemnly, "I can get out of there, which means outta here, a lot faster. And I've *gotta* get outta here, sister, because if I don't, either he's gonna kill me or I'm gonna kill him."

It was true. More than ever, the old man had a hate on for Tim. "Disloyal little bastard," he growled again and again, "rather go out with that grinnin' fool of a damn silly bugger Scandihoovian dimwit than with his own father."

Cassidy figured what stuck worst in the old man's craw was that Tim had made enough money he didn't need anything from him, he could pay for it himself. To compound what the old fart saw as the insult, they all knew Tim didn't even have to stay. If he needed a place to sleep and food to eat, he could walk onto the troller the same as if it was still fishing season, and Einarr would grin and reach for the coffee pot. Then boot the old man's arse if he came storming and blustering to try to collect his kid. Or even bat him on the head with a fishkiller, stuff him below, take him ten or twelve miles out and drop him over the side. That was something else about Einarr Gunnarson, something everybody knew or claimed to know. You don't bugger about with him, he might smile a lot but Jesus he runs deep.

Cassidy couldn't figure it out. She knew if she had tried to stay with Aunt Joan and Uncle Gillam, all hell would have cut loose and stayed cut loose. Cops, court orders, you name it. But Tim could have got up from the supper table, grabbed his jacket and moved onto the troller, and the old man would swallow it. He might choke doing it, but he'd swallow it. The bigger puzzle was why Tim didn't do just that.

He'd changed in the two months and a bit on the boat. There was no more sniping and nattering about helping, he cut kindling by the cord and stacked it where it would stay dry, he kept the wood box filled without needing to be asked or told. As soon as he saw her starting some chore or other, he was right there helping, and when the old man ragged on him about doing women's work, Tim scared the very spit out of Cassidy. Her mouth actually went dry, her throat tight.

"What it is, you see," Tim said evenly, not looking much like a not-quite-thirteen-year-old, "is even if I'm a kid, I don't have to worry about dishwater making me not a man. The only thing that's gonna fall off in the suds is the stuff on the plates and forks."

She thought the old man would explode. She was so scared little whimpering noises came unbidden from her throat.

"You talk like someone who thinks he knows something," the old man managed. "And all you're doin' is blowing hot air out your asshole."

Tim grinned. The old man turned away, and Tim let him have the last word. "That's all you have to do, I think," he told her later. "Just let the old fucker think he's had the last say-so."

"Don't swear like that."

"Sorry, sister."

That's what he called her most of the time now. Not Cassidy, not Cass, not Sis. Sister. There was something formal about the way he said it, something polite and almost foreign. Something their kind of people didn't do. It pushed her to stop calling him Timmy and make sure she called him Tim, or Brother.

Sometimes he'd look at her and smile and she wanted to

grab him in a big hug and tell him how much he meant to her, but she didn't do it. She didn't have to. He knew.

"What a pair of dipsticks," the old man sneered. "Just lookit 'em, side-by-each at the table readin' their damn brains into train oil."

"Either they're awful smart," Tina laughed, "or awful stupid."

"They ain't smart, you can be sure of that."

But it was worth any number of nasty remarks and insults because by helping Tim with his homework, Cassidy was actually improving her own marks because she *had* to keep ahead of her baby brother. It would be unbearable if he caught up to her. She had always known more than him, and she wasn't going to sit reading detective magazines while he caught up to her and maybe even passed her.

The old man was messing around and they all knew it, but only Tina gave the first part of a good goddamn about it. "Just let me find out who it is," she raged, "and I'll rip her hair out."

"Not likely," he mocked her. "You couldn't rip the feathers out of a dead chicken."

"I mean it, s'help me God I do. I find out that floozie's name and I'll knock her damn block off."

Cassidy had to agree with the old man. Tina wasn't in any shape to take a round out of a starving kitten. But Tina didn't seem to know that, and she lurched from bar to bar to bar trying to catch the old man with his new squeezie. In one of the bars someone must have looked at her sideways, or maybe not looked at her at all, and she lost her temper, started ranting and raving, lifting glasses of beer from other people's tables and hucking them wildly. Of course the bouncer called the cops. And of course when they showed up nothing would do but Tina chuck a few glasses at them, too. She was kept in the pokey over the weekend and went up in front of the magistrate Monday morning, hungover and looking like shit on a stick.

The magistrate might have done any number of things, but he looked at the wreck standing defiant and ridiculous in the courtroom and instead of sweeping her under the carpet like so much dirt, he ordered her sent to hospital until such time as they felt she was in fit shape to appear before him again. That took a month, and nobody went up to see her the entire time. When she faced the judge again she looked almost alive. He told her a few things, and she hung her head and nodded. She was sent off for three months.

When she came back, it was as if nothing had happened. She walked in the back door and for a minute Cassidy didn't know who she was. Three months of regular meals and no booze at all had worked a miracle.

"So," Tina tried to joke, "did you throw out my stuff, or what?"

"I didn't throw anything out, it's where it was when you left."

"Your old man still messing around with that floozie?"

"Which one?" Cassidy laughed softly.

Tina laughed with her. "Yeah. Right. You figure he's been messing around on me all along?"

"Why not? You've been messing around on him for as long as I can remember. He no sooner starts up the boat motor than you're cat-assing like there was no tomorrow."

"I should kick his ass is what I ought to do."

"Maybe he should kick yours, too. Near as I can see you're two of a kind."

"Oh lah-de-dah and hoity toity!" But Tina wasn't mad. She didn't even seem ticked off.

She ate enough supper for three people and chatted away as if she'd been off on a luxury cruise instead of sitting behind bars. The old man looked as if he didn't know whether he was supposed to chew and swallow his food or the plate it was sitting on.

– VIII –

Cassidy wakened feeling thick headed and half-slept. She wanted to go outside and pee, but before she did that, she cleared the ashes and placed small dry sticks on the few remaining coals. The sticks browned, then sent out wisps of smoke before the first flickers of flame licked tentatively at the weathered grey bits of beach cedar. She added larger twigs, and finally some chunks of broken wood and even a few pieces of bark, and when she was certain the fire was established, she left her womb and hurried to the hole she had dug.

It wasn't until she started to pick her breakfast that she realized her fingers were swollen and skinned, the tips of them raw and sore. So much for writing the story of your life on solid rock.

She chose mussels instead of oysters. They were easier to pull free. These weren't the small mussels which grow on every pier piling, wharf, cliff-face, rock, stick and piece of garbage touched by the tides, these were not the ones which clustered on the rusting metal frames of vandalized shopping carts or mounds of discarded or abandoned logging equipment, these were the huge blue ones which used to be abundant and which, thanks to pollution, are no longer abundant.

She picked eight of them, some as long as the palm of her hand, and put them around the fire. The dark blue shells, some of them with barnacles growing on them, opened slowly, exposing the deep gold meat inside. The contrast between the near purple of the shell and the bright flesh was almost startling. Cassidy had expected grey, like oysters and clams. When she picked up the first one to eat it, she noticed the shape of the creature she was about to eat. She looked carefully, touched it with her sore finger, then blushed, recognizing what she was seeing. The shape, the lips, the delicate foldings were so exquisitely vulvic it was almost like looking at herself.

For the briefest moment she hesitated, then she ate the meat and thought she had never tasted anything as good— even the oysters she'd eaten the day before. Chewier and drier than oyster, richer and very satisfying, she could probably eat them every day of her life and not get tired of them. "Whoever designed you," the sound of her own voice startled her, "did a good job. You look lovely and you taste . . . like coming home to a warm house full of friends."

She put the second one near the graven wall. If the rock, or whatever, was eating, it didn't seem right to give only that which Cassidy herself couldn't eat or didn't want. Sharing seemed better.

She had thought she would be able to eat and eat and eat but the golden meat was rich, at least as rich as scallop or abalone, and she was full after the third mussel, stuffed after the fourth. She took off her clothes and left them in the hoochie, then went outside and walked into the water for a good swim. It wasn't the same as a nice hot bath, with scented soap and honey-and-almond shampoo for her hair, but it was there, and it rinsed away the sweat and sleep, and took the sand from the creases where it had hidden itself—with every intention, she was sure, of rubbing her raw.

She left the water more quickly than she had intended when a seal surfaced nearby. Too close for comfort as far as Cassidy was concerned. She remembered all too well those other ones, the males with the enormous whangs. Wonks. Dinguses. Peckers.

The thermos was still three-quarters full and the coffee was still hot, and she drank two cups of it while sitting on her shirt in the hoochie. The cigarette she smoked made her dizzy at first and she realized she was almost weaned already. Without being aware of it, she had cut back on the smokes and now, so quickly, she was back where she had been when she first started.

"Don't worry," she told the rock spirit, "I'm not going to quit, there will still be the chance for you to enjoy the smell. You can share with me, if you want," and she leaned forward and passed the cigarette in front of the wall. Michael would have said it was the movement, the draft, that made the glowing tip brighten, but Cassidy knew what it really was, and she accepted the knowledge without feeling silly, self-conscious or scared.

She wondered how long it would take her to go totally insane trapped on this big black islet, this overgrown boulder. No trees, no grass, and so hot she didn't dare sit outside for long. She must have been mad to sleep on that flat outcropping, to not even think of taking the time to find a bit of shade. She might well have boiled her brain and died of cerebro-soup-itis. Maybe she had. She hoped not. She wasn't sure she wanted to spend eternity like this. Maybe it was a way station, a little clearinghouse, a place where the dead went to be judged. Maybe thoughts like that were the signs of boiled brain syndrome.

She heard them barking and looked outside, her heart pounding, her belly cramping with fear. There they were, lazing in the shallow water, and she had never seen such big seals. Maybe the ones in the open ocean were bigger than the harbour seals. The barking seemed to be directed at one particular one which was hauling itself onto the beach.

Cassidy didn't dare go outside, didn't dare make any noise. She hoped the damn things couldn't smell as well as dogs could, prayed they wouldn't all come up on the rock and sniff out her hiding place. If she had any reason to believe they'd rip out her throat and kill her in seconds she might not be so terrified, but she had seen those gross wonkers, had seen what they did with them. And she knew it was as awful a way to go as any she could think of. What if those women hadn't died? What if they had survived the attack? What then? Had they found salvation rocks, as she had?

Or had they turned into seals themselves?

Stupid thought, that. It's only in old fables and legends that things like that happen. Smarten up, Cassidy!

Her sore fingers began throbbing. If that wasn't something. Huddled in a rock and driftwood hoochie, surrounded by animals she knew were killers, scared out of her wits, and what bothered her most was some sore fingers. So much for the stories of people who survived terrible danger and only later, when they were once again safe, did they realize they had walked miles without knowing their leg was broken. They had to be better people than she was. Oh well, and if she did get screwed to death, at least the story was there. She had a book in her condo, one she had bought in the Book Store, a book with pictures and text about the petroglyphs, those strange rock carvings found in many places on the coast. She wondered if those strange shapes had been put in the rock the way her life story had, people with sore fingers leaving their history. She wasn't sure why people did that, wasn't sure right now why she had done it.

She looked at her wall. The writing was still there, deeper than ever. It wasn't until she started to read it that she realized it was different. If she hadn't already been terrified by the presence of the seals, she might have been frightened by the marks on the wall.

Nobody with any choice in the matter would have gone into the ground to hammer and claw for coal, so the hapless were made to be miners. The ones who wanted to sell the black rock for profit paid sojers and poliss to provide them with workers. The mercenaries simply grabbed anyone who looked capable, roughed him or her up significantly, then hammered a wide metal collar around their neck.

Anyone found harbouring someone wearing a collar would wind up wearing one, too. It was forbidden to give any kind of help to someone with a collar, forbidden to hire them or even feed them. They were forbidden to use public roads without a pass signed by the one who had appointed himself their owner. They had no rights at all except the right to live in the most meagre of shelter, and to die early deaths in unsafe pits where the air was foul with poisonous gas and the shafts collapsed without enough warning for them to flee to safety.

Their children were doomed to join them in the dark as soon as they were able to walk to the pit head. To ensure they didn't somehow smuggle their children into the care of relatives, the owners collared their known family, too. In the off-chance any member of the family owned anything—a small farm, perhaps, a weaving shop, a fish boat—laws were passed which made it illegal for them to own property.

People who did not live in those areas which produced coal had no idea at what cost their houses were heated, and had they known they may not have cared. They were warm, or at least marginally so, and someone had to do it.

Raven was born in the pits. Her mother worked dragging the stone boat until the cramps became too strong and she couldn't move her legs for the pressure of the child being born. She fell to the uneven floor of the shaft and lay gasping until the contraction eased. Then she crawled into a small room abandoned because of poor output, and there, safe from the stone boats and sledges of others as miserable as herself, she gave birth to her third child. She couldn't see in the darkness, she had nothing with which to cut the umbilical cord, there were no swaddling clothes, no bassinet, she didn't even know people had such things. She gnawed the cord with her teeth, wrapped the baby in her own shirt, and lay as mute as the coal seams and rock faces while her blood dried and crusted on her legs and belly. An hour and a half later, she was back at work. When the horns blew signifying the end of the shift, she stumbled and lurched her way to where the child lay snuffling and wailing and, in the darkness, unwrapped it, put her shirt back on, and tucked the child against her own flesh. Then she joined the file of stooped and exhausted workers trudging their way to the cage which would lift them from this wet and vile hell.

She saw the baby for the first time by the light of the small cooking fire in the mean hovel she shared with her parents, her brothers and sisters, and the tired young miner now considered to be her husband, who was possibly the father of the baby. She called the baby Raven because she was so black.

Not only was the little body covered with coal dust, her head was covered with a thick cap of dark hair.

Even if she had had the time and energy to cuddle, to snuggle, to sing lullabies and croon, she wouldn't have done it. She didn't know how. Nobody had done any of that with her, and she had never seen anybody do it. Besides, she had already given birth twice before and seen both little boys die within the first week. She didn't dare love this infant girl. If you loved them, it hurt too terribly when they died.

She cooked supper, a pot of oatmeal, and ate hungrily when it was ready. No milk, no honey, nothing but the boiled oatmeal. At least there was as much as she wanted. Often there was hardly enough to stop the grinding pain in her stomach.

She slept with the child, and her exhaustion was so thorough, her sleep so deep, that it was up to the baby to find her breast and suckle. If she couldn't do that, nuzzling like a puppy or a piglet, if she couldn't squirm herself into position and get her mouth on the swollen nipple and suck milk into her body, then best she die now than later.

When they trudged back into the pit for their shift, Raven was tucked against her mother's skin, held close to the breast by a broad band of cloth. It was just a band of worn drab cloth, not the family tartan. None of them had the wherewithal to purchase such a thing. Most were disinterested in such things anyway, and some were ignorant of which clan they could claim. That was no accident. It served the ones who considered themselves to be masters, because if there was no clan there was no group to claim their loyalty, nothing outside their death sentence reality to beckon to them. They could accept the metal collars and the misery, or they could die.

But they died whether or not they accepted their slavery, and they died years sooner than the ones who, however poor, however starved, still lived in what they thought was freedom. The masters didn't care if they died, there were plenty of others out there who could be grabbed, knocked about, collared.

Raven grew up in the gloom of the pits. By the time she was three years old she was picking up bits of coal and tossing them into the cart. When she was six she was given a small-headed, short-handled pick and it was her job to lie, with all the other children her age or older, in the damp and mud on the shaft floor, and hack away at the seams of coal. She pick pick picked a hole big enough to crawl into and keep hacking, and as the bits and chunks fell, she passed them back by scooping them under her belly, then scrabbling at them with her feet. When only her feet protruded from the hole, her own father grasped her by the ankles and pulled her to him. The sharp edges of the unhewn coal scraped, scratched, cut and gouged into her back, and her blood mixed with the rubble beneath her belly. She cried out, often screaming with pain, but the sound was muffled by her own body and by the rock and coal entombing her.

Once she was out of the hole she had made, her tears leaving streaks in the thick dark on her face, she and the others scooped up handfuls of coal dust and patted it on the cuts to stop the bleeding. The scars, when they formed, were like bluish snakes tattooed on her shoulders and back.

And before she had stopped crying, she was down in the sodden muck again, pick pick picking at a new face, making a new hole, and a child older and larger than herself was enlarging the one Raven had just exited.

Six days a week, and on the seventh, because the word of

God must at all times be obeyed, they attended compulsory chapel. The good grace and kindness of the master had intervened to the extent that chapel did not start at the same time the shift usually went into the pit. They actually got to sleep in, although to what time nobody knew because they had no clocks and wouldn't know how to read them if they had.

In chapel they were reminded there would be a place for them in heaven only if they lived good and productive lives, honoured God, obeyed their master and were properly grateful for the kindness he showed by providing them with the chance to worship. You will be known in heaven for good work done here on earth.

Raven was eight when her mother died lying on the muck slick floor of a hole begun by Raven herself, died giving birth to her seventh child, a girl who was also dead when Raven found her mother. Of the seven children, Raven, her brother Tamas, and her little sister Mary alone had survived past infancy. But Tamas was crushed under tons of coal and slate when the roof of the room he was carving came down on him, and Mary died of bad air when her pick broke into a gas pocket.

Raven had her first child when she was fourteen. She named him Tamas, after her brother. She wasn't sure who the father was, he might have been any of the several who had grabbed her in the darkness, forced her against the wall of the shaft or onto the muck of the floor or into one of the rooms she had cut open. The first few times it happened she fought, kicked, bit and even screeched, but after a while it was easier to save her strength and just let it happen.

But she knew she wasn't going to spend her entire life in the muck. After chapel she often sneaked away from the grim huddle of shanties and made her way to the hills overlooking the pasturelands where the master's fine horses grazed. She didn't know to envy him or to resent the wealth she had no choice but to provide for him. She just sat, feeling the breeze on her face, nursing her vow that she would not wind up the way her mother had. When she was dying of black lung before her thirtieth birthday, her children Tamas, Mary, Edna and Jaime carried her to the hill and, because she commanded them to, left her there and returned to the hovel they called home. She died alone, coughing blood, fulfilling her own vow to herself that whatever it took, she would not expire in the stinking dark.

Not one of her children knew anything about reading or writing, or anything else beyond their own mean existence. They did not know there was something unfolding called the Industrial Revolution. They did not know that far to the north, great changes were happening. The north had never been worth the time or effort of invading, of subjugating, of dividing among the masters; the north was cold and wet and home to heathen highlanders who lived by what means they could find. The soil was too poor, the climate too wet and cold to grow much by way of garden, but there were hills and moors where wild animals could be hunted, and streams, rivers and lakes where fish could be caught, and the people lived and survived, independent and as wild as the creatures they hunted.

But the new equipment made it possible to distill liquor on a grand scale, and whiskey was gold. Whiskey-making depends on plenty of good water, and the engines ran on water. The engines also required coal to turn the water to steam. And so land that had been considered worthless for centuries was suddenly desirable because of the water on it, the coal beneath it. The masters sent their mercenaries north.

It took years, it took death and it took the pouring of blood, but in the end the mines went down, the dams went up, the whiskey barrels moved south and the defeated were collared and sent into the mines. They had no idea how to cut the coal and little inclination to do it. Skilled miners were sent north to demonstrate the proper way to mine, and to set a good example.

Examples were set, to be certain. And one of the ones who learned well was Raven's daughter Edna, who ran for the hills and tried to hide herself with the tinkers, gypsies and cairds. For her efforts, she was hunted down, caught, whipped until she was close to death, and then branded. If she'd had any sense at all she would have learned, but as soon as she could walk well enough to be ordered back down into the mine, she ran off again. When they caught up to her the next time she was pregnant, so it was decided to hold off whipping and beating her until after the baby was born. They locked her in the stocks as an example to the others, but somehow, and nobody could ever be found who had seen or heard a thing, the stocks were wrecked and Edna was gone. Years later when the poliss and military surrounded a group of highland rebels, Edna was recaptured. There was, however, no sign of the child. Or children. Edna refused to answer questions, and when she was beaten, she cursed and roared insults; when she was branded again, she spit at the one with the red-hot iron, and when they cut the big tendon leading to her heel, she cursed them all, every one of them.

She went back into the mines, limping and dragging her ruined foot. Even she knew there would be no more running away for her, no more sneaking off and making her way to the wild ones. Even she knew she would never again see the children she had borne, and had protected by fostering them with crofters who had been allowed to stay on their land. She had paid for their care by sharing with the ever-hungry family whatever hares and grouse she could snare, whatever fish she could catch. She had seen her children running in the sunlight, she had seen them growing straight-limbed and straight and strong, if a little skinny. And she knew she would not see them again.

She waited, but not passively or idly. And then the time came when the gas began to fill the shafts and Edna went daft—or so the master preferred to think. She began throwing chunks and bits of coal at the others, yelling at them to get the hell away, get out, *go*, damn it, and many of them did. Those who didn't go perished with her when, with a wild shriek, she struck a piece of flint against the metal of the coal cart. The explosion ruined that section of the mine.

Daft, they said. Daft, they were told to say. Daft, they were taught. But they whispered to themselves of the ghosts in the mine, of the woman who walked the shafts talking of rebellion, of the laughter that echoed in the rooms. And they whispered the stories she had told them, of grass and tree, of stream and sea, of stars, moon and blessed, blessed sunlight.

Cassidy didn't like the story. She felt cheated. Where was *her* story? She'd wound up with raw fingertips and her story had been replaced by a different one, and a dreary morbid one, at that. She would have walked out of the hoochie, but she could still hear the seals barking and quarrelling, and she wasn't so miffed she'd risk her life just to make a point. Anyway, she didn't believe the new story. She had never heard anything about metal collars, or about needing a pass to go out on the road. She had learned about the Industrial

Revolution in school, about James Watt and his mother's steaming kettle, and no word about any of this dreadful rot.

She leaned against the cold wall and shivered. Suddenly, all she wanted was to be away from here. Not just away from here but back in her own little apartment, her condo, her home. She wanted her nice new furniture, she wanted a good hot bath, she wanted a big Dairy Queen cone, dipped in chocolate. Was she going to spend eternity here, on a rock, cowering like some damn coward, hiding from a pack of fish-breathed seals and living a life which was no life at all? She had daughters, she had granddaughters, she had a freedom she'd never known in her life before, and all she had to do to get back to it was risk certain death. And hadn't she been risking exactly that each and every night she had dared to close her eyes and go to sleep next to a person who thought nothing at all of rearranging her face, breaking her bones, holding her by the throat and choking her until bright lights danced inside her head and all she could hear was the hollow echo of his voice shouting threats? She'd never get back if she just sat here! You don't get anywhere at all if you won't move.

Cassidy took her time. She carefully packed her things, few as they were, in the backpack, and put on her clothes, or what was left of them. And then she risked her life. She walked out of the chucked-together shelter. She had no idea what she was going to do or how she was going to do it, but she knew why she was going to try. If one woman can blow up a whole mine shaft in the name of freedom, another woman can take the chance of getting past a few seals.

The seals stopped their racket and turned their heads slowly, staring at her with round, round eyes. Cassidy was so frightened she was sure she was going to pee. The biggest of the dark-pelted creatures opened its mouth and she saw pointed teeth, big pointed teeth, big sharp pointed teeth, and her knees began to turn to butter. Surely she would collapse in a trembling heap.

"I'm going home!" She hated her voice. Thin, trembling, so obviously the voice of a quivering wreck of a jam-tart. "I don't know how, but I'm going to try."

The open-mouthed threatening yawn changed, and Cassidy would have sworn on every Bible in the Anglican congregation that the animal was trying to smile. She couldn't have sworn that the shape of the creature began to change, or that for a brief moment she was looking at a person, not a seal, and she would never dare tell anyone that even as she felt herself rising inches from the ground and moving through the air, toward the tips of the waves, she saw a naked woman walking down the small beach, toward the hoochie, carrying several oysters in one hand and a half-eaten egg salad sandwich in the other. And Cassidy wouldn't even admit to herself that mere seconds before, the woman had been one of the pack of seals. Some things just don't bear thinking about. A person might go right around the bend.

In some small way, she recognized what was happening. It was like the dream where she looked down from the ceiling and saw herself lying asleep in bed, curled on her left side, always on her left side. In the dream she could fly, no flapping of wings, no Superman posture with the arms extended as if diving, just up and off, as fast or as slow as she wanted. She would leave the bedroom, leave the house and suddenly be outside, in the night, moving without even the swish of the wind, looking down on streets she recognized, seeing from above houses she passed when she drove or walked when she was doing errands.

Only there was no street, no road, just the water, and she

couldn't gain the height she had managed in her other dream. Her feet were no more than half an inch above the tops of the waves, and she couldn't seem to zip or zoom or soar as fast as she chose, she could only manage this steady forward motion. She supposed she was dead on the beach by now, ripped to shreds, bits and pieces of her sitting in the stomachs of the carnivores. But she didn't feel dead. She didn't even feel as if she was dying. She felt like a woman who was moving from one place to another, through thin cool air.

She had no concept of time, but she was profoundly aware of everything else around her. The sky above was a pale, pale grey, with whitish-grey clouds in puffy layers, except on the southwestern quadrant where they looked like big fluffy feathers, ostrich plumes perhaps. Three cormorants sat side by side on a floating log, watching her. She wanted to wave to them but she was afraid any movement would dump her into the sea. Dimly, the half thought came that there had been four of them sitting on that log. Where was the missing one? Was it true Japanese fishers caught baby birds, collared them, then taught them to catch fish and take them back to the boat? With what did they reward them? What a rip-off! What a wretched rip-off! Imagine diving down, hell-diver swift, swimming underwater, beating what were wings in another place and what were next best to flippers here, and then *snap!* a fish in your beak. Up, up, up with the fish, up and to the boat. Hands reach for the fish. And what do you get? A rice ball? A slice of sushi?

They'd probably tried more than once to train seals to chase schools of fish into the waiting nets. The wolves of the sea were too smart for that one. No rice ball for them. But if they wanted to, if there was a reason they could respect, how easy it would be, and how lucky the fisher so blessed.

And then her feet were touching the sand, and she lurched and stumbled the way everyone does when they come off the escalator. Fine gravel and bits of dried seaweed and broken shell crunched under the soles of her damp sneakers when she walked up to where the grass began, bleached yellow by the sun. She had no idea where she was. No idea at all. But at least she wasn't where she had been, and that was something. She might as well think of it as progress.

– IX –

She had expected to land in the place where she had first embarked on the Zodiac, but she could see she must be somewhere else. In front of her were benches set into clean cement, with wrought-iron legs and seats of moulded white plastic. Just back of them were swings, a slide, and flowers growing in boxes set on large pieces of twisted driftwood. To her left were houses, many houses, mostly large single-family ones sitting on yards that were almost no yard at all. They had balconies and bits of patio with barbecues built of brick, and except for the colours of the trim, they were so like each other a person could be forgiven for thinking them first cousin to mushrooms, springing up by the hundreds after an autumn rain.

To her right, past the small park, were more houses, less elaborate, some of them tri- or four-plex and some of them apartment buildings. They were less elaborate, with the kind of barbecues you could buy in any hardware store, mostly with propane bottles nestled underneath and little fake-cedar shelves and counters surrounding the metal tub and lid. Cassidy could see cars, too, sitting under sundecks, and she realized she hadn't seen any cars at the more expensive places. They must have underground parking.

What struck her as even more odd wasn't the lack of cars near the pricier houses, but that there wasn't a dog to be seen or heard, nor any evidence on the ground that any had ever passed the place. And there weren't any children. Nary a one, as Aunt Joan used to say. Not chick nor child, nary a one.

She started walking, past the playground without children, past the flowerbeds, along the wide blacktop central access drive toward what she hoped would be a road or a highway. The tarvia led her to another roadway, past houses and more houses to yet another wide black strip. This one had yellow lines down the centre of it, which meant it was a highway, she hoped. In the distance she saw what she thought and prayed was a gas station. If she could just get to a phone, things might start to look up.

Ten minutes' steady walking and she was standing staring at the most automated set of gas pumps she had ever seen. Buttons here, more buttons there, all a person had to do was punch in how many gallons of what sort was wanted, then slide a plastic card into the slot and no need for a human attendant. Where were the stations where you got a smiling face, a cheery word, your windshield cleaned and your tire pressure checked?

She looked for a human being and saw a small booth, but it was empty and the door was barred and locked. The washrooms were open, though. She went into the one with the stylized picture of a woman in a dress, and did what she could with hot water and some heavily perfumed pink powdered soap, possibly the most unnatural colour she had seen.

If she hadn't known the face staring back at her from the mirror was her own, she might not have recognized it. Her skin was dark with tan and windburn—and probably, she thought wryly, a fair coating of dirt and campfire soot. Her hair was the same silver, but longer. She made sure the door was locked from her side, then stripped off her faded jeans and tee shirt and, with a wad of sodden paper towelling for a washcloth, she scrubbed the salt, sand and dirt from her skin. What she wanted was a long hot soak in a deep tub, but for now, this was like heaven, the water in the basin hot, the soap garish but effective. When the water got to looking grey she emptied the basin and refilled it, and continued her sponge bath.

When she picked up her tee shirt, a fine drift of sand and salt fell to the clean tile floor. She tossed the shirt into the basin and washed it thoroughly, then put it on, wet as it was. She should have used her tee shirt for a wash cloth, she thought, it might have done a better job, not left bits of shredded paper stuck to her skin.

The tattoos on her arm were more noticeable with the dirt gone. The lines were intricate and fine, the colours clear and bright. Her nails were badly in need of a good filing and shaping, but at least most of the dirt under them was gone. Come out in the wash, Auntie Joan would have said. Oh, never mind, it'll all come out in the wash.

She checked her pack. Her thermos was there, and when she removed the lid she could see it was still three-quarters full of coffee. She still had a full pack of cigarettes, and plenty of money in her wallet. She would have used some of it to leave a tip if there had been any sign of someone to collect it.

She went back outside and looked in the small booth, but it was still empty and the door still barred. No use waiting. She set off down the highway. She had very little idea of where she was going, but anywhere would do, and if she could just find out where she was she could try to get in touch with Mikey and Cori. They'd know what to do! Cars whizzed past her, some heading in her direction, some going back the way she had come, but nobody even slowed, let alone stopped, and before long Cassidy got tired of standing hopefully, thumb out like a supplicant. To hell with the lot of them, she'd walk.

It wasn't long before she saw a strip of road curving from the highway to the right. She almost started down it, but the only marking was a small green sign with a number, 43, and no name of a town or any hint of it, so she ignored it and just kept walking. There were other turnoffs, some to the left, but she ignored them, too. She wasn't going to 43, or 44 or 45 either, and she sure as hell wasn't interested in going to 57.

After a while the muscles in her legs began to ache, and by nightfall she was limping. She sat on the side of the road with a cup of coffee and a cigarette and tried to make sense of things. None of it fit together. It was like that dream where she just kept walking and walking and walking, getting nowhere, with no idea why she was on the move or what she was leaving behind or where she was going, just walking. "If I had any damn sense at all, I'd do the feet-off-the-ground trick," she mumbled.

And as quickly as that, she was sitting a good twenty feet above the road, still cross-legged, still with her pack on her back and her thermos lid of coffee in one hand, her cigarette in the other. Maybe she *was* dreaming. But if it was a dream, it was a good one. She could feel the breeze cool on her skin, hear the slight swish of air past her ears, and see the traffic moving below. She doubted anyone down there could see her. After all, she'd been as good as invisible when she was trying to hitch a ride.

From up here she could see that the trees on either side

of the highway were not, as she had supposed, the fringes of a forest. They were merely decoration. Beyond them were houses, lots of houses, and she could have taken any of the turnoffs and been minutes away from stores, telephones and nice soft motel beds.

Well, better late than never. She thought herself down and she was down, standing on a sidewalk, with a 7-Eleven all-nighter beckoning ahead of her. And next to it, a motel.

She went to the motel first. The young man tried hard to hide his reaction but she knew he didn't think highly of her appearance, of her, or of the idea of renting one of his units to her. But she had cash, and he wasn't about to argue with that. He gave her the key and pointed toward the unit.

It was exactly what she had been expecting, exactly what she wanted. A big bed, a TV, a bathroom, a small kitchenette. Almost home! But before she used any of it, she went to the 7-Eleven and got supper: smoked meat sandwiches, fresh glazed doughnuts and two small containers of milk. She also got a hairbrush, comb, toothbrush, toothpaste, shampoo, conditioner and skin cream. They had souvenir tee shirts in plastic bags and she chose several, a blue one with a picture of an eagle, a coral pink one with a picture of a wolf and a grey one with an osprey. She looked for one with seals, but there weren't any. On a shelf immediately below the tee shirts was a pile of socks, from which she chose several pair of thick cotton white ones. It was too much to hope for underpants, jeans, new shoes and a jacket, but tomorrow wouldn't take forever to arrive and she could get them then.

When she left the store she was munching one of the smoked meat sandwiches. The taste of the spices was delicious and her mouth watered. She wanted to gobble them down, consume them in one or two huge bites. When she thought of the milk in the waxed cardboard cartons her throat tightened. She wanted to rip the top open, drown in milk, spill it over her chin, pour it on her head, rub it into her skin.

Back in the motel room she sat on the sofa gobbling her food, the phone receiver propped between her shoulder and her ear, holding the sandwich in one hand and dialling with the other. She tried Mikey's number first, and a recorded voice droned, "The number you have dialled is not in service." That almost stopped her cold, but she clicked the receiver button and tried Cori's number. This time she got an answer, but it wasn't Cori, it was a man, and he sounded impatient. "You've got the wrong number," he scolded. "I've never heard of this Corinne. You'd better check your directory!" And he hung up.

It was as good a suggestion as she'd heard for a long long time. The only problem was that when she tried, the directory assistance operator told her there was no listing for Mikey, or for Cori. Not even a business listing. And that did stop her, cold. Surely to heaven Cori, a practising cosmetic surgeon, would have an office number. But there was nothing. Fear clutched at Cassidy. She began to feel as if she was going start screeching.

Instead she turned on the television and surfed from one channel to the other, finally landing at the news channel. Troop movements in the Middle East. More troop movements in the Gulf. At least Southeast Asia seemed quiet, that was something. She ate hungrily, only half watching the screen. Too many things made no sense. And since her brain obviously wasn't going to be much help right now, she concentrated on making her body feel comfortable. She ate her sandwiches, then every one of her doughnuts, and washed it all down with the milk. The whole world and the shreds of her life might be in total disarray, but at least her stomach was happy.

She tried the directory assistance again, just in case, but the directory had not changed its mind. No Mikey, no Cori. Cassidy gave up and tried for a listing for Maria. No luck. Almost ready to flip right out, she started in on her half-siblings, but there was no Freddie, no Peter, no Janet.

She gave up. She was shaking with fear, her face slick with tears she did not know were falling, and the only thing she could think of to do was to take a bath.

She stripped off her clothes while the water was flowing into the small tub. She stepped in, sat down and let the hot water rise. Bits of paper towelling still clung to the skin on her belly, although all that walking had shaken them from her legs. She leaned back and ran her wet hands across her skin.

Suddenly she felt as if the sand from the beach were trapped under her eyelids and all she wanted was to go to sleep. She sat up, turned off the taps and began to scrub herself with the thick cloth and the tiny bar of motel soap. She rinsed soap from her skin, pulled the plug and stepped out of the tub. The towels were white and much used but they got her dry. She pulled on one of her new tee shirts and stumbled to the bed.

She dreamed she was in the hidden section of the big house, in one of the libraries, desperately looking through books. Volume after volume she picked up and flipped through rapidly, skim-reading, then closed the book, replaced it and picked up the next one. Book after book, shelf after shelf, hour after hour, and when she finally wakened, she knew things, new things, and knew them to the marrow of her bones.

Things like:

Selkies or Sealkies or Silkies are capable of leaving their seal skins behind and walking on earth as women or men. They often live with or marry humans, and have children who are both human and not. The women are beautiful, the men have enormous organs, and both female and male have almost insatiable sexual appetites.

Time spent in faeryland is not the same as our time; a few minutes of faery time can be the equivalent of days or even years of regular or earth time.

Those who stumble into faeryland, or who are washed there by the sea, should not eat faery food or they won't even think of leaving until everything in their own life, their real life, has changed, and time has passed, passed, passed.

Faery food is easily recognized: the loaf of bread which is never consumed, the jug of water or wine which is never emptied. (The oysters, Cassidy thought, which although picked are never gone, the thermos of coffee which doesn't drain, the cigarettes which don't vanish no matter how many of them you smoke.)

She knew other things, too.

Tim, her brother, had become an old man and died. Her daughters had lived their lives fully and died. Maria had grown old and died. Liberty and Freedom had grown up, married and had children, and their children had had children and those children as well and even Cassidy's grand-daughters had grown old and died. Her great-grandchildren knew little about her other than a story that she had been lost at sea, and their children knew even less.

No use wasting time mourning the dead, it was over and done with years and years and years ago.

She was well and truly on her own.

She realized she knew nothing about what had happened to Michael. And didn't care, either. In fact she hadn't thought of him in the longest time.

She sat on the edge of her bed, feet dangling, trying to digest her new knowledge.

Gone. All gone. She was alone, totally and completely alone. She was alone in a world she had never imagined, a world where the last of the once-blanketing forest had been reduced to a thin strip alongside the roads and highways, which had multiplied into a clogged network. When she tried to think what the rivers would be like, her mind spun unproductively.

It wasn't what she wanted. So she was alive, so what? The price was too high. Okay, it was her own fault, all she had thought about the entire time she was on that black rock was getting away from it. She hadn't concentrated on going home, she hadn't fixated on getting back to her family, she hadn't focussed on her granddaughters, she hadn't given a thought to where she might be going. All she had aimed for was leaving. Well, she had left, all right. She'd have been better off if she'd stayed. At least she wouldn't have had a mind full of emptiness.

She supposed she could kill herself. And wasn't that a wry turn, she'd struggled so hard not to die and now dying seemed like one of the better choices. But how could she do it? She had a niggling feeling she'd be wasting her time if she tried to drown herself. If she had survived the cold waters during a fierce storm she would probably just bob like a cork out there, drinking the endlessly hot coffee and smoking the continuous supply of cigarettes, and eventually going so loonytoons she'd start chatting with the three cormorants on the log. She had no idea how to get a gun, and blowing out her feeble brain seemed a messy leave-taking. But it would be easy enough to slit open the veins in her wrists and ankles.

Except she didn't want to. It would probably hurt, and she had never enjoyed being hurt, it was too much like what she'd been doing all her life. Just letting things happen. Drifting. Oozing along through her own life waiting for some Other to fix the ragged edges and mend the holes. She had thought she was past that passive non-living, but look at the jackpot she'd landed herself in just by not taking a firm stand. Come to think of it, how firm can anybody's stand be when they're drifting on the breeze with their feet off the ground?

Well, damn it! She'd just go back and try. If at first you don't succeed, try, try again. Return to Go, do not collect a hundred dollars, and while you're at it, forfeit Reading Railway and Marvin Gardens.

She wasn't surprised in the slightest when her motel room door opened and the selkie woman—the same one Cassidy had seen walking down the beach as she was carried off over the water—walked into the room.

"Do you mean it?" the selkie asked.

"I won't live without them." Cassidy had never heard her own voice sound so determined. "If I can't go back to fix the mess, I'll go back to the black rock, but I won't go any further into this."

"Oh, well then," the selkie smiled, and her teeth were like any person's teeth, or at least like any person wished her teeth were—white, even, and with the tiniest of spaces between the front ones. Not the least bit pointed, nothing to indicate that in another embodiment, this woman was a carnivore. "Think about it. Make sure you know what you want. You," and the smile faded, "are becoming a pain in the ass."

"I'm very sorry, I'm sure," Cassidy apologized, struggling

against the urge to laugh. "But really, who asked you to intervene?"

And like *that*, there she was on the parking lot of the marina, her car keys in her hand, unlocking the door of the Tracker. She was still wearing her life jacket and her backpack awkwardly strapped on over it, and she was positively drenched.

Down at the edge of the launching ramp, where the concrete pad sloped into the water, people were pushing aluminum boats from shore, other people were running with a Zodiac, and someone was yelling something at her.

"I swam!" she called. "That's all I know. I was wearing my life jacket and I swam."

She supposed the police would trace her through Mikey's licence number and arrive on her doorstep with questions, pens and little notebooks, but she didn't care. Right now all she wanted was to get to the motel and get warm.

When she walked into the motel room, the heat was on and a hot supper waited for her on the table in the kitchenette. It was fish and chips, of course. Selkie hovered, eyeing the meal impatiently and hungrily, which seemed only to be expected.

"Start without me," Cassidy suggested. "You don't want it to get cold and I'll be a minute or two getting out of this wet riggin's."

Selkie nodded, but made no move to start eating. Cassidy went into the bathroom, stripped off her wet gear and tossed it into the bathtub, then stood under the shower until the blue tinge was gone and she had stopped shivering. She wrapped herself in her blue terrycloth robe and went back to the other room. Selkie was still waiting, the fish and chips still pleasantly warm, although no longer hot.

"God, that smells good." Cassidy sat down and reached

for the malt vinegar. Selkie sat, eyes bright with anticipation, nodding agreement.

"I'd like to leave as soon as we've eaten." Cassidy spoke around a mouthful of deep-fried cod. "I don't want to tell my family what happened over the phone and I sure don't want them to see it on TV." Selkie nodded again, busy with her fries. "Would you mind if I introduced you as . . . oh, I don't know . . . a friend I met on my trip? That's true, actually, isn't it? And I think it would help if I knew your name . . . so I can introduce you."

"Selkie."

"And the last name?"

"Last name?"

"The name of your family."

"Selkie."

"I'm sorry, I can't just introduce you as Selkie Selkie, they'll think I've got a rare brain disorder that has me repeating myself, myself. How do you feel about Finnegan?"

"Finnegan?"

"Sounds good to me. If anyone asks, you're Seale Finnegan."

"Do you know how to make tea?"

"Tea? You want tea? No problem," and holding a piece of delicately browned cod in her fingers, Cassidy rose from the table and went to make tea.

Seale sipped carefully and a look of such total bliss came on her that Cassidy felt shy. It was almost like watching someone else reach orgasm. Not that she herself had much experience in orgasm.

In the car, driving through the rapidly gathering night, Seale sat stiffly, only her faith keeping her from leaping out with a shriek.

"You haven't been in a car much, have you?"

"I was in it driving from the beach to the motel. You didn't drive as fast that time."

"Nobody drives as fast in town as they do on the open highway."

"Oh. Does this thing go faster than this?"

"You want to go faster?"

"No! It's too fast already."

"God, driving with you is like driving with Cori! I'm doing the speed limit, okay?"

"Limit?"

"Limit. Cori and I have a slight disagreement about that. She says the limit is the absolute fastest a person is allowed to drive. I think it's more of a suggestion of what the minimum ought to be." But the weak joke escaped Selkie completely. "Do you do this often?" she asked, searching desperately for a new topic. It seemed that talk, however meaningless, might help make sense of things, help keep her from having to examine what felt like a bad case of delirium. Maybe she'd swallowed too much salt water. Maybe any amount of salt water was too much.

"One time before."

"And what was that like?"

"Oh, it was nothing like this. I watched him, out in his boat, fishing. Every day he would leave the land and go out and place his nets. He had yellow hair and blue eyes and he laughed. And I followed him. I waited until he went to bed and when he was asleep I went into his house and got in bed with him. He thought he was dreaming." She smiled, and again Cassidy felt as if she were spying or eavesdropping. "In the morning he was puzzled, and started to ask questions. I told him there were things I couldn't tell him, things he mustn't ask me, personal things, and he said he would respect that. Every day he would set his nets and I would become my other self and chase fish into them. But he didn't know that. At night, when he returned, I would already be at the house, cooking supper, with a length of cloth on the loom. He thought I was a weaver. We had two children, and they both had hair and eyes like his. But then he began asking questions. What did I do while he was out fishing? Why was it his mother had gone to visit and I wasn't at home, even though she waited for me? Where did I go when I wasn't at home? Who did I meet? What did I do? In the end, I left him. I had to."

"And the children?"

"Why, they went with me, of course. Although later, much later, one of them decided he preferred life on the land, and went back to live with his father."

"But you got to visit with him?"

"Oh yes, he would dive into the water and become who he really was, and together we would chase fish into his nets. He became quite wealthy. He married a landwoman, and had children, and one of my grandchildren was one of us. The others," she sighed, "had no idea who they ought to have been. Oh, they were fishers, that was something they had grown up knowing how to do, but they only knew the half of it."

"My brother and daughter are fishers."

"Yes. Tim and Mikey."

"You know them?" Cassidy gaped.

"Only to see them."

Cori opened the door, saw Cassidy and grabbed her in a strong hug. "You look wonderful!" she gushed. "You must have had a good holiday, you look so rested and ready to take on the world."

"It's been a trip, all right," Cassidy laughed softly. "This is my friend Seale Finnegan, I met her on the beach," and that wasn't so much a lie as a slight editing of what might or might not have been the truth.

"Glad to meet you, Seale. Come in, come in, I'll make coffee. Tell me about your holiday, tell me everything."

"Actually, we aren't going to stay long." Cassidy walked into Cori's apartment and felt less at home in it than ever. "I just didn't want you to hear the big news from anyone else. And I wanted you to see for yourself that I'm fine. Never better." It was true.

"What news?"

"The Zodiac tipped."

"What Zodiac?"

"I went out to go whale watching and the Zodiac tipped. They're still looking for the others."

"You're kidding! Oh God, Mom, you could have been killed!"

"You could slip getting out of the bathtub."

"Tell me all about it!"

"There isn't much to tell, Cori. The Zodiac tipped, I got thrown out, I was wearing my life jacket, and I floated. Bobbed around like a cork. And then, I don't know how, I was within sight of land and I swam and . . . here I am."

Cori turned to Seale, who sat quietly on the sofa, patiently waiting for the coffee Cori hadn't even started to make. "Were you with her?"

"No. I didn't go whale watching."

"My God, Mother! What are we going to do with you! A woman your age going out in a little rubber boat."

"Don't be silly! A woman my age made it back to the beach, it's the younger ones are still out there!" She almost said more, but caught herself in time. "Where's that coffee? You promised coffee. And I have to tell the girls. I don't want them learning about it on the news."

"The girls will be in bed, sound asleep. Maria never watches television news, she says all it shows are people dying and she's seen enough of that for one lifetime. But you'd better see if the marine operator can get hold of Mikey and Tim."

The connection was bad, the static thick, and Cassidy had to shout to be heard on the other end, but at least she was able to tell them what happened, answer a few questions and reassure them she was fine. "You try to stay out of trouble for a while, okay?" Mikey's voice was faint, and she sounded as if she were talking from the bottom of a deep well. "We'll be home in a couple of days and I expect to see you with both feet firmly planted, okay?"

"I promise, dear. And you too, you hear?" Cassidy knew how to get Mikey off her case in a hurry. "You know I worry about you out there, especially now that I've seen for myself just how chancey it really can be."

"Don't you get started, Mom. I'll see you soon. Gonna sign off now, okay?"

Seale grinned and Cassidy wasn't sure if it was because she'd figured out exactly what Cassidy was doing to defuse and deflect Mikey, or if it was the smell of the coffee and cream puffs Cori was bringing.

When Cassidy wakened, she wasn't in Cori's living room drinking coffee and eating cream puffs. She was in her hoochie, and what had wakened her was the silence. Not complete silence, she could still hear the waves crashing on the black rock, she could even hear the sand swishing against itself as the water receded. She could hear rain falling too, and a trickling sound as the rain ran from the inadequate slapped-together driftwood pretending to be a roof over her mean shelter. But the barking, hooting, yapping and fish-breath chortling of the seals was gone. With a little bit of luck, they would be gone too.

She felt her way along the damp rocks to the slit she had been thinking of as the doorway, and looked out into the wet black night. She might as well have kept her eyes closed. Hot tears slid down her face and a huge sob welled up in her chest and burst loose. She fought it down. If even one sob escaped her, she would cry until she died.

She moved carefully to where the small fire was supposed to be. The sand was hot and the ashes still warm, and fumbling in the dark she managed to push gently until she was rewarded by the gleam of a few coals. She managed to get the coals bunched together, then laid dry grass and some beach twigs on them. Blowing carefully, trembling with fear and cold, her mind racing over and over with the same ridiculous prayer, Oh please, oh please, oh please, after what seemed an eternity, she finally was rewarded with a few weak flames.

Cassidy was still muttering Oh please, oh please, oh please when she put cedar bits on the tiny fire. The cedar caught almost immediately, and her prayer changed from Oh please oh please to Thank you thank you thank you. Now she could see enough that she could carefully choose from her small pile of hoarded firewood, and more carefully than she had ever chosen groceries or furniture, she picked her pieces and added them.

– X –

By the time she was able to relax enough to lean back and enjoy what she had made happen, Cassidy was shaking, and not just with cold. She hadn't gone anywhere! She hadn't lifted from the pull of gravity and floated easily back to safety, especially not twice. She was right where she had been, and still groggy from her hours of too-deep sleep. Tim had marvelled at her ability to turn off all things unpleasant, crawl into bed, and sleep in spite of the yelling, the crash of overturned furniture, the rant and rave of angry drunks. "You could sleep through an invasion," he had teased.

Michael had been scornful of the same quality. "No sense, no feeling, I guess," he had said bitterly. "Sleeping Beauty herself. When all else fails, escape to dreamland and let someone else cope with the real world, eh Cassidy?" But she had never slept through the sound of a baby waking, had never, when the girls were small, fallen into that sodden place that left her mouth feeling thick with fuzz when she wakened. She had always been able to live in the moment for them, with them, although any time they took a nap, so did she, and only the sound of their voices could waken her. She knew that kind of sleep was an escape, and she wondered if narcoleptics shared her condition but hadn't quite yet learned to control it. First sign of fear or boredom and *boink*, they dropped right off.

She wasn't a bit surprised to see the rock walls were nothing but plain rock walls. Stupid of her to have wanted to believe she could use her fingertips to carve her life story into the stones. Things like that just don't happen. Except in dreams and fantasies.

But all the things she had wakened from her dream knowing, she still knew. She knew about faeryland and faery food, she knew about selkies and about other things, too. And she knew time was not, as some people said, a river, one you could only jump into from where you were, then float in one direction, downstream. Time was a lake, an ocean, and you could jump into it anywhere and swim purposefully off in any direction, or all directions at once. But you didn't float effortlessly into it, you had to swim. You had to take an active role, you had to participate vigorously or the only thing that would happen after you launched yourself would be that you drowned. Drowning in time, what a crazy-making way to die!

Cassidy didn't just leap up and race out to fling herself into the chuck. She did what she could to organize herself. She stuffed her clothes into the little pack but left her thermos of coffee and cigarettes next to the collection of empty oyster shells. "You never know," she said aloud. "And I know at this point I know nothing." Something, or someone, had kept the thermos full of hot coffee, and someone, or something, had kept the cigarettes replenished. So why deny the evidence of your own eyes? You can Believe even when you don't Know. The proof? Flip the light switch. The bulb brightens even for those who don't know why or how. Otherwise, only electricians and electrical engineers would have working light bulbs.

She waited until the door hole became apparent, then took her pack and went outside. The rain had become drizzle, the sky was overcast, but she could see the lighter side of the sky where the morning sun was at least trying to shine through the clouds. So that had to be the east. Unless the entire world had gone topsy-turvy, and there was no guarantee that hadn't happened.

Every kid on the coast knows if you stand with your right hand pointing to the east your left will point to the west, and your face will be turned to the north and your bum aimed at the south, where the Yanks live. Well then, there it was, and she at least had some idea of direction.

She shrugged on her life jacket, zipped the front and did up the security snaps. Then the backpack. Nothing much in it now, except a pair of jeans, a tee shirt and her wallet. She had no idea at all where her other stuff had gone. She was almost certain she'd had a nice warm sweater. A nice warm heavy sweater. Or was it a jacket? Well, she didn't know, she couldn't remember. Just as well, it would probably weigh a ton when it got wet. She might have to get rid of her pack for that very reason. In fact, the more she thought about it, the less sense it made to burden herself with stuff. She took the pack off again and opened it. She took out her wallet, put it in the little side pocket of the life jacket, and pressed the velcro strips together tightly. She almost threw her pack away, but then went back to the hoochie and placed it next to the thermos and the cigarettes. "Someone might need it." She felt stupid talking to a rock, but nobody laughed so she couldn't have been too far out of line.

She felt ready, then. Ready to swim or sink, ready to do or die. She walked into the bitterly cold water, turned her face both south and west, and walked in up to her chin. She kicked off, her arms reaching, and she began to swim for her life. Before the sun set on that first day, Cassidy had determined that if she ever managed to get anywhere, one of the first things she was going to do was write a letter to the life jacket manufacturers. Dear madams and/or sirs: Thank you so much for making such an excellent product. I recently had unwilling occasion to depend on one of your life jackets and can say without hesitation or fear of contradiction, it saved my life. Enclosed please find a thousand dollars. Please use it for something nice for your workers, chocolates, maybe, or a new coffee machine for their lunch room. With sincere regards, etc. etc.

She didn't intend to sleep. In fact she had promised herself to stay awake, because she didn't want to drift back to the black rock or another just like it. But she fell asleep, rocked by waves, giddy with the exhaustion of kicking and stroking, kicking and stroking. When she wakened she had no idea where she was. For all she knew she was exactly where she had been when sleep claimed her. But the sky was clear and she could see the sun, so she started swimming again.

The second day was hell. Her body was so stiff and sore she wanted to wail and she dreamed she was in heaven, with a tall glass of lukewarm chlorinated and fluoridated tap water and two extra-strength pink Arthritis Pain Formula pills which she knew would make the hurting stop. Except there was no tap, no water, no pain relief, just the swimming, and when she could no longer use her arms, she continued kicking until her legs just flat out would not move, could not move. Then she bobbed.

By the morning of the fifth day she was exhausted, dying and angry. Where were all those goddamn fish boats, power boats, houseboats, sailboats, ferryboats, tugboats, tramp steamers and oil tankers? She hadn't even seen a measly rowboat! Where was the Coast Guard, where was the Air Force, where was somebody, anybody at all? It wasn't as if she was thousands of miles out in the middle of absolutely no place on earth, she was practically within touching distance of the shoreline! What about all these damn waterfront properties, condo developments, where were they? Where were the damn marinas, the boatels, the fishing charter lodges? "Hey!" she croaked weakly. "Hey, you!" but nobody answered.

The sound of her own voice jarred her. So did the pain in her parched, salt-seared throat. She tried to swallow but there wasn't even the hint of a drop of spit left in her mouth. Salt was crusted thick on her lips, and they were swollen and starting to split. It was just bloody stupid, to die within arm's length of the damn beach! It wasn't fair. She had tried so hard, and now she was going to die right here where the water from the small creek mixed with the sea water, swirling colder-then-warmer around her legs.

"Hey!" Her echo bounced back at her from the bush. "Hey, you!" Her last shred of sanity flickered feebly, and instinct moved her legs. Cassidy swam painfully, desperately, and then, when her arms and legs scraped against the rocky bottom, she crawled, wriggled and squirmed her way up out of the sea, to fall belly down, face turned to one side, in the shallows of the creek.

The fresh water lapped at her face, her tongue moved, her throat convulsed and, weak as a newborn rabbit, Cassidy managed to drink a few ounces of unsalted water. Hours later, she drank more. Sometime during the night she crawled out of the creek and lay on the grass, and probably God herself didn't know if Cassidy was asleep or unconscious.

Birdsong wakened her. She sat up, her head pounding bloody thunder. Every inch of her body throbbed. She hurt so much she knew she was alive—if this was death, nobody would ever die! The awfulness of it would drive them back to life. She groaned, inched her way to the stream, then drank. She could taste something metallic in the stream water, something that reminded her of when she was young and had put a penny on her tongue.

No rock cluster, no hoochie, no matches, no fire, no clothes, but surely there would be oysters somewhere, and clams, probably. She didn't relish the idea of eating them raw, but beggars, as they say, cannot be choosers. She really didn't feel up to trying to rub two sticks together to make a fire.

She found berries. Blackberries. Well, there you go, that's the good old coast for you! Blackberries. That meant it was probably August. Salmonberries, now, aren't going to be your calendar, they're the first berries but then they just keep coming until well into September, so what kind of a calendar is that, tell you where you are in time—somewhere between spring and winter. Huckleberries came after the salmonberries and they too hung on until the fierce gales were blowing, no calendar there. But blackberries are pretty much time-specific.

Except Cassidy could remember one year when she had actually found a ripe blackberry as late as the twentieth of October. Of course that was one of those El Nino years, but still, little guy or not, on Thursday, the twentieth of October there was a ripe blackberry, and Cassidy had eaten it. It was a bit sour, unlike these big, thumb-sized Himalayans, soft and juicy and at times too sweet, too full of sugar. No wonder the bears will walk on broken glass to stuff themselves!

She slept again, lying with her head on her life jacket, her arm shielding her eyes, her body bare but for her dingy underpants. The sun warmed her body, the horrible shivering spasms passed, and when she wakened no more than an hour later, she felt so much better she smiled. "Thank you," she said, and it didn't matter to whom she said it.

So here she was. Here. So did she sit on her backside until the blackberries were finished, did she head up or down the shore, or cut off across country?

She wasn't going far from the creek. There were too many miles of coast without streams or creeks. Besides, berries grow better near water!

Cassidy followed the little creek, pausing at berry bushes and replenishing herself with salmonberries, huckleberries, blackcaps, thimbleberries, even Oregon grape and salal berries. Of course the more of them she ate, the more often she had to stop and allow her body to rid itself of the salt water she had swallowed, and get rid of the berries too. "Worse than green apples," she muttered, wishing for a roll of toilet paper. Never mind all the survival books with their ideas for using moss or grass or leaves. Nothing beats toilet paper!

She could hear cows, and crows. Even before she stepped out of the bush she knew where she was. "Oh, thank you," she breathed.

She started from the brush, then stopped, frozen and staring. Coming toward her was herself, as she had been how many decades ago? Young Cassidy, vibrant, full of hope, strong-bodied and more attractive than Old Cassidy had ever thought she was.

Her grade seven teacher, Mr. Fox, had warned her. Watching her zipping around the bases in a lunch hour softball game, he had laughed, then said, "You move so fast, my dear, that one of these days you'll meet yourself coming back." Well, you were right, Foxy. You were right about almost everything else.

Cassidy sat down and thought about things. Thought hard. So many choices! If she stayed in this here-and-now she could change everything. She could make sure to meet herself, make sure to expose young Michael, save herself, both her selves, her old self and her young self, from all those years of abuse and servitude. And then what? Well, no Mikey, no Cori, no Freedom, no Liberty.

Unthinkable.

Or she could wait, let things go as they had gone and then appear when Cori was an infant. She could step in then and change things. But to change any part of the dynamic would be to change the Cori and Mikey to come, and then they wouldn't be the same as the ones she already had, somewhere. Sometime. She liked her daughters. Liked the toughness of them, the humour of them, the loyalty and love of them. Change them? Not at all.

She had to think, damn it. This was no time to get sleepy, this was no time to sit at the bole of a maple and snooze. If no Mikey, or at least no Mikey-as-she-is, then no Liberty and Freedom. No thank you to that one, too.

She wakened in the womb. Seale had oysters baking on the rocks around the small fire, and she lit a cigarette and handed it to Cassidy, then poured her a cup of hot coffee.

"I'm very sorry," Cassidy said, and meant it. "I seem to be fumbling it."

"Last chance," Seale told her.

"Could I please talk things out with you? It seems I think better if I can actually hear myself doing it."

"Talk away. I *love* it when people talk. As long as they're talking and not just yammering on about nothing."

"If I start to yammer, tell me. All right, I have infinite choices here. The big one is already made, I think. I would like to go back to my life as it was before I decided to go whale watching."

"So what about . . . ?" Seale waved her hand at the walls of the womb.

"I want the pictures there. I want the writing there. I believe it. Every word. Every story."

Who was it had written that if even one woman told the truth about her life the world would shatter? Smart woman. Wise woman. Deserves the Pulitzer Prize or the Nobel. Hell, give her both! We all have the true history of the world engraved on the walls of our womb, there since before birth. Even hysterectomy cannot remove the truth of who and what we have been and are. For the rest of her life, Cassidy would pay close attention to those stories.

"I would like to come back here, in dreams, perhaps, or maybe for real, I leave it up to . . . whoever. I want to read those stories, time and time again, remember them, memorize them, maybe write them down for my granddaughters and great-granddaughters."

"Now, are you *sure* you know what you want?"

"Yes. I want my life as it was before the little rubber boat capsized. Because if I change anything at all, I won't be who I am, I won't have what I have, and worst of all I won't know what I know. And," she smiled, "you have worked so damn hard to teach me."

"Well . . . " Seale smiled. "You are, after all, the grandmother of my granddaughters, and they deserve the best."

The grandmother of her granddaughters. Cassidy wasn't

the smartest woman on the face of the earth, but it didn't take her long to figure it out.

"Mikey?"

"Beautiful Mikey. Tough Mikey. Wonderful Liberty and Freedom."

"And you're their grandma?"

"Aren't I lucky?"

"Yes. But so am I. Lucky that Mikey decided to continue having me in her life. I suppose she could have—"

"She wasn't even tempted. Oh, she and my son are very good friends, and she often dives over the side to visit. Tim understands. He never gets upset. But from the very first visit, there was never any doubt that Mikey would return to land. Return to you. We all hope that one day soon the girls will come for the summer holidays. Perhaps one of them will choose to stay in the sea. Perhaps not." She grinned. "You know what you people say—you win some, you lose some."

"Imagine! My granddaughters are magical!"

"So are mine."

They laughed together, and for the first time in her life Cassidy began to believe that anything—*anything*—was possible. All she had to do was get on with it.

"What about the others in the boat with you?"

Oh, God. Choices, choices, choices. She didn't answer right away. She thought, really thought hard. "I'm not sure they are any of my business," she decided. "If the boat doesn't tip, well . . . too much will change. Or not change. And maybe we have to learn to let people make their own mistakes, even if they are life-threatening. Oh, I don't know!" she said helplessly. "I really do not know."

Seale moved the cooked oysters to a place in front of the carved wall, poured the coffee from the thermos into the sand, put the cigarettes and the little white lighter near the oysters, then crawled toward the doorway. "Come on," she said. "Get a wiggle on, will you?"

Cassidy woke up in the motel, the sandwich wrappings in the wastebasket, the empty milk containers on the bedside table. Seale was curled on top of the other bed, naked, not even a bedsheet or coverlet over her tanned skin. Cassidy stared, enjoying the sight of so much smooth skin, the curve of breast, the strength of thigh. If the males had such ginormous throbbing dinguses, what did the females have? She couldn't see much difference between the body she was enjoying watching and her own. Maybe the difference was . . . passion. She'd like to try a bit of that, herself. God knows there had been a dearth of it in her life so far. Like rain in Texas, something a person could hear about and never experience.

She lay for long minutes watching Seale's gorgeous breasts as they rose and fell with her breathing. Had anything ever looked so beautiful? Had anything ever invited, even demanded, soft touch, reverent stroking? It occurred to her that the dip of waist perfectly fit the shape and size of her own face, and the swell of hip would fit the palm of her hand.

She knew Cori would make coffee and serve cream puffs, she knew she would talk to Mikey on the radiophone connection. She knew more. She knew when Mikey walked into the room and saw Seale she would know . . . *know* . . . the core truth of everything. Would Cassidy blush? Were there things you didn't want your daughter to know? How stupid! You spend your life trying to teach them that great trick of standing with both feet firmly planted on the ground while reaching for the stars, so why draw the line at a little out-of-control passion?

Mikey would look at her, move to her, hug her hard, hard, as Mikey always hugged. She would know. Mikey always knew. She would look at Seale, and the grin would start. She would cross to her, fold her in a hug, even introduce Seale Finnegan as Liberty and Freedom's other grandmother.

Cori would be puzzled, but not for long. After that, there was no telling how she would react. Waters run deep, and Cori's ran deeper than most.

The price tag might be obnoxiously high, however. Life wouldn't be just one passionate encounter after another, it never was. Day-to-day began to intervene. Would Cassidy be able to hold her tongue on all the questions, all the where-were-you's, all the how-could-you's, the how-am-I-supposed-to's, and the why-would-you's? Would she be able to accept the inevitable absences and not be consumed by jealousy? Easy to say we are who we are and what we have is what we have, but saying isn't doing. There are always price tags. Some of them are just too spendy.

She got up, pulled on her worn and faded jeans and her poor sad tee shirt, tired socks and nearly finished sneaks. Moving softly she put her magic wallet in her back pocket, the motel room key in the left front one, and without so much as bothering about her silver hair, she left.

She walked past the twenty-four-hour store. Then stopped and thought of the tee shirts. Even if they didn't have one with a seal on it, the others had been fine. A bit pricey, but everything has a price tag, hadn't she just had a long talk with herself about exactly that? What is worth, anyway? A person could decide something was worth a buhzillion dollars to her, and be unable to find anyone else willing to pay more than a dollar sixteen. Something some people take for granted can mean life or death itself to other people. A thing is "worth" only as much as someone else is willing to pay. And if you're willing to pay that, then there's no way it can be "too much."

She went back to the twenty-four-hour store and got her tee shirts. They even had one with a picture of a seal, but it was an ordinary seal, not a selkie. Ordinary seals have lovely eyes and "cute" faces, but the sensuousness is missing, except probably to other seals. A selkie, now, even if sunning itself on a rock with a dead fish half out of its mouth, is more than merely exotic, it is erotic. Ask someone who knows! She paid for her tee shirts and left the store smiling. Half a block farther down she saw a Workwear World and went in. Mikey did most of her clothes shopping there, and Mikey always looked just great.

Cassidy moved past the displays, fingering the cotton shirts, the soft jackets and vests. She supposed if she made up her mind and insisted that was the way it had to be, she could be sure Mikey would recognize Seale, move to her, call her Mom, acknowledge her as Freedom and Liberty's grandmother. But did she have any right to lay down dictum? Shouldn't some things be left to Mikey to decide?

And what about clothes for Seale? Much as Cassidy would enjoy driving down the highway with a sensuous naked woman beside her, she could all too vividly imagine the number of in-the-ditch cars, pickups and transports she would leave behind her. Fender benders galore! The tracks ran parallel to the highway for several miles. What if the engineer looked over, saw Seale, and forgot why he was sitting in the cab? Did he actually steer the thing around the bends and curves, or would it manage them on its own? And if he was there to steer, what a sight that would be, the train continuing in a more-or-less straight line, off the tracks, across the road, into the toolies, the engineer slack-jawed and bug-eyed, for-ever unable to make anyone believe what he had seen. And what of the traffic cops? Would their cars spin, spin, spin like tops, spin as the whirling bubble gum machine on top flicked the lights, would they spin, spin, spin, sirens burbling, until they ran out of gas?

She could choose some things for Seale. Enough to get her covered so she could find a store and go in and choose for herself.

Was that what the whole involved and convoluted go-round was about in the first place? Leaving everyone room to choose? But only for themselves, not for everyone! Such a thin line between choice and dictatorship. Scary. But then, what wasn't? If a person got into it, just getting out of bed in the morning could be terrifying.

She didn't suppose a good drenching would stop any of the wars. Armies were always willing to slog through the mud for the chance to blow up or incinerate unarmed women and children. Glory glory glory, flags and banners, marching bands and spit-and-polish boots, change the old country-and-western song from cowboys to soldiers. Mothers don't let your sons grow up to be soldiers, or your daughters, either. But a few good drenchings might relieve some of the desper-ation that makes guns and uniforms seem like some kind of future. She wondered if she would have to go to Africa, or if she could soak the place by wishing, the way the wishing and worrying had put out the forest fire. And Australia, there were places there where not a drop of rain had fallen in twenty-five years. Well, she'd always wanted to see a duck-billed platy-pus. You never know, it might turn out to be Seale's cousin.

If she let the cat out of the bag she could get rich, rich, richer than anyone could believe. She toyed with the idea while choosing a tee shirt for Seale. She could get paid to go to dry places—Australia, Africa, Texas, Ethiopia, you name the drought-stricken place and she'd go, getting paid in gold or jewels or both. Once the word got around, she could probably get paid even more *not* to go to places. Disneyland would be good for several mil a year. Plenty of jam from Knotts Berry Farm. More wheat than she'd know what to do with if she timed her visits to Saskatchewan properly.

How much money did a person need, though? And more to the point, what *was* money? Already she had this wallet that never quite emptied, how much more would she ever need? She didn't suppose the time would ever come when she would feel satisfied with just a loaf of bread that was never eaten, a flagon of wine that was never emptied. No, she'd want some blackberry jam, some smoked salmon, some whipped cream in which to dip her blackberries and raspberries. But the wallet would ensure that, as would her own juice-stained fingers, because one thing she knew she was going to do, beyond the shadow of a doubt, was pick pick pick the berries spread out on what someone was bound to call "wasteland," there for anyone to pick and to enjoy. Yes, berry picking, from June through to the twentieth of October, if she was lucky.

Anyway, she didn't *have* to get paid to drench Africa. She could just do it. She didn't *have* to be remunerated for going to Australia to listen to the kookaburra. She knew, as well as if she had already experienced it, how much satisfaction she would get if she climbed to the top of Ayer's rock and stood, surrounded by sand for miles in every direction, and then, to the amazement of all and sundry, the rain began to pour.

It was true, if one woman spoke the truth about her life, the world would shatter. It was also true that if one woman chose the truth about her life, the world would begin to put itself together again.

Aunt Joan had told her the truth. Aunt Joan had never lied to her. It was a choice Cassidy made herself that had made it impossible for her life to be as full and joyous, so far, as Aunt Joan. And why had she never before realized just how absolutely gorgeous Uncle Gillam had been? His eyes, for example. Round, and startlingly blue. Too many years had passed since she had seen them, too many years since she had sat with her cousins and enjoyed being silly. He whose name she no longer wanted to think about had done everything he could to isolate her. Well, she could break that isolation. They wouldn't ask questions she would be afraid to answer, they wouldn't dump recriminations, they knew all too well the why and how of it, had known long before Cassidy had realized things herself. She could choose to change that. She *would* choose to change that. And her half-sisters and half-brothers? How could there be a "half"? How do you add, subtract, multiply or divide blood when all of us are cousins? Whether you call her Mother Eve or First Woman doesn't matter, her children were siblings, their children cousins, and we are all of us her grandchildren, so we are all of us cousins. And the barriers between us are of our own creation.

Ah, such a lovely shade of blue! And a design on the front, the magical dogs, legs and tails intertwining, tongues whorled and spiralling. Dogs, animal of the earth, not of mere dirt and rock but the earth, protecting the generations, doing the bidding of the Old Grandmother, the source of birth and death, of rebirth and death. The dogs of the sea, the wolves of the sea, the dogs of the earth, and Seale's body moving under the fabric, curving out, dipping in, inviting, no, demanding, touch, of hand and tongue, of heat and passion. And jeans, but what size?

She stood by the shelves of folded jeans, looking at tags. Waist so much, inside seam so much, 28-32, and 32-34, even 48-26, well, scratch that one, for sure. No Goodyear blimp, no Pillsbury doughperson. She closed her eyes and called up the vision of Seale lying naked on the bed, and even if she hadn't actually touched her, she knew, she *knew* and reached unhesitatingly for the exact same size as for herself. Odd how she had never before thought of herself as sensuous. But if Seale was, and if Seale was the same size as Cassidy, then wouldn't it stand to reason? They said things equal to the same thing were equal one unto the other. They said. Hmph, who were "they," anyway? She had never thought of herself as erotic, but then she had never stood in the middle of a store full of clothes and been able to see, more clearly than she saw the work gloves and woollen socks, a body that made her mouth go dry and her stomach lurch.

Less than fifteen minutes later she came out with everything she needed except sneakers and underwear. She walked down the sidewalk, and in the plate glass windows she saw her own reflection. Silver hair and eyes so bright they seemed to dominate her face. Until she smiled, and then the smile was dazzling, all those new teeth, probably. Or maybe just the growing inner happiness. "Just." Oh, just that.

She went into WalMart and nearly got overloaded by more stuff than a person could imagine needing or using. But past the tons of plastic kitchen gadgets, past the heaps of fake India rugs, past the mounds of imported plastic sandals, the lingerie department. Cotton, of course, and just try to find it. More nylon, thislon and thatlon than enough and one little easily overlooked selection of cotton underpants. She could hear it now: Oh, all you have to do is look at the sales figures and you'll see that for every six pair of cotton we sell six hundred pair of shitslon . . .

Rich burgundy-coloured cotton for Seale, pale blue for herself. Usually her underwear was white. Functional. Bland. Blah. Not this time! And purple! By God, yes! Purple, dark and light. And green, too, the clear blue-tinged green of the sea, the sea which had saved more than just her life, more than just an ability to suck air in and shove it out again. Saved it all. All. She looked at the bras and knew Seale needed one the way Anywoman needed another nose on her face. She reached for one for herself and then dropped her hand. No. For crying in the night she was a woman with tattoos on her arms and around one ankle, there was no way she was going to put up with the itch, with the rubbing, with the red marks on her shoulders or the way the snaps dug when she leaned back in a chair. And so *what* if nobody else in WalMart seemed the least bit aware of the intricate tattooing? Their loss, not hers. It wasn't there for them, it was there for her, to remind her of who she had been and would be again, and to honour. Above all, to honour.

Sneakers. Her own looked as if someone had been swimming in them in the salt chuck for days, then stumbling along rocky beaches for more days. She supposed there was no use in deciding to boycott (womancott) any of the big-name brands because of the foul way they treated their workers. In all likelihood most of the others were made in the same sweatshops, guarded by goons with machine guns. Where would a person get shoes not put together with slave labour? Could one find shoes made in countries where generations of drought hadn't starved people into working in hell holes? Maybe she could do something about that. In the meantime, any old brand would do as long as they fit. And a same-size pair for Seale, always with the understanding she might prefer to go barefoot.

Cassidy paid for the underwear and shoes, left WalMart and decided never again to go back. Too cluttered. They tried so hard to make it seem as if they were a friendly store, they wound up looking like robots. There *had* to be what used to be called Mom and Pop stores left. Just about every town in the world has one or two families known for being stubborn. If she couldn't immediately put a stop to slave labour, she could at least decide not to give her money to the huge chains which were part of bigger chains, which were in turn part of corporations, multinationals and transnationals, with more wealth and power than many nations, and less commitment to people than any dictator.

She stood in front of a display window and stared at the musical instruments as if she had never before seen anything so absolutely gorgeous. Each and every one of them reminded her of curve of thigh, of breast, of belly. She grinned, mentally scolding herself for being a dirty-minded old biddy, and then she laughed aloud. No wonder the puppeteers worked so hard at invalidating elders! A person fumbles and bumbles and wanders into and out of just about every mistake that can be made, and just about the time she learns which end is really up and which other ends aren't and never will be, the ones who dictate everything from fashion to public opinion spread the slander about senility and dementia. They have to. It would never do to show respect to those who have finally learned not to pay any attention to the plastic kitchenware, the plastic underwear, the plastic non-degradable and totally degrading tit-holders and moulders. If the elders get away with it, and get respected, the youngers will soon catch on and ignore the crap as well, and then where would the profit be? Heaven's sake, we might even stop shitting in our drinking water. What a concept!

Cassidy knew then, even as she laughed at her own silliness, that she hadn't made any mistakes at all in her life. Not really. She had done what she had done, and even if it looked as if marrying old wotzisname had been a huge error, it wasn't. She got Mikey and Cori, and Freedom and Liberty, and the price had been cheap. She had done what she had done, and it must have been the right and proper thing to do because she was alive. Alive and nowhere near as stupid as she once had been. She wasn't smart yet, there were trips to take and things to learn before she even began to be smart, but she wasn't stupid, and she never had been.

By goddess, she knew what she knew. And better yet, she Knew what she Knew.

She stopped at a deli and loaded up with mouth-watering goodies, stopped at the convenience store for two quarts of coffee cream, then hurried to the motel.

She unlocked and opened the door and went inside, suddenly grinning. Seale was sitting cross-legged on the bed where she had been watching television, but she turned and saw Cassidy grinning at her.

"Food," Cassidy said, but meant something else. "Drink." She held out the cream, but offered more. "Clothes." She knew she wouldn't be putting any on until later. Much later.

"Welcome," Seale said, her meaning clear. And Cassidy had a damn good idea what it was the magical females had to offer.

The fiction of ANNE CAMERON

ANNE CAMERON's novels and short stories have won her a devoted following. In her fiction, Cameron probes the most intimate spaces of the woman's world—the toil and pain of parenthood, the tidal surge of sex and desire, and the boundless wonder of the human imagination.

THE WHOLE FAM DAMILY
An unwilling grandmother to kids raised with poverty, violence and fetal alcohol syndrome, even a woman as strong as Isa sees that she can't fix the whole fam damily all by herself.

One family's cycle of violence, poverty and addiction . . . rings powerfully and disturbingly true. Ottawa Citizen

. . . both breadth and sharp detail in her evocation of working-class life . . . an admirable novel. Globe and Mail

Novel ◆ 6 x 9, 264 pp, pb ◆ 1-55017-134-8 ◆ $17.95

DEEJAY & BETTY
While trying to save a child from the pain they endured, two victims of childhood abuse meet, and transform their lives.

Novel ◆ 6 x 9, 264 pp, pb ◆ 1-55017-112-7 ◆ $16.95

A WHOLE BRASS BAND
Jean's just about had it with kids, in-laws and, well, family. "If bullshit was music," she tells her dog, "they'd be a whole brass band."

Novel ◆ 6 x 9, 304 pp, pb ◆ 1-55017-075-9 ◆ $17.95

ESCAPE TO BEULAH
A feminist fable for our times, told with a dispassionate, fascinated vigour. Vancouver Province

Novel ◆ 6 x 9, 234 pp, pb ◆ 1-55017-029-5 ◆ $16.95

BRIGHT'S CROSSING
Cameron understands the way a woman's work affects every other sphere of her life. Feminist Bookstore News

Short Stories ◆ 6 x 9, 184 pp, pb ◆ 1-55017-022-8 ◆ $16.95

KICK THE CAN
Cameron knows how women talk to each other. Vancouver Province

Novel ◆ 6 x 9, 160 pp, pb ◆ 1-55017-039-2 ◆ $15.95

SOUTH OF AN UNNAMED CREEK
. . . joins courage to comedy with a light, sure touch. Ottawa Citizen

Novel ◆ 6 x 9, 200 pp, cl ◆ 1-55017-013-9 ◆ SPECIAL $6.95

WOMEN, KIDS & HUCKLEBERRY WINE
Witty, entertaining and strangely uplifting. Edmonton Journal

Short stories ◆ 6 x 9, 258 pp, pb ◆ 0-920080-68-5 ◆ $16.95

STUBBY AMBERCHUK AND THE HOLY GRAIL
A novel about baseball, high-stakes poker, women's wrestling, and growing up, all served up with a bit of magic.

Novel ◆ 6 x 9, 282 pp, cl ◆ 0-920080-22-7 ◆ $22.95

Available from better bookstores or
Harbour Publishing
Box 219, Madeira Park, BC Canada V0N 2H0
Phone (604) 883-2730 ◆ Toll-free, BC only: 1-800-667-2988
Fax (604) 883-9451 ◆ E-mail: harbour@sunshine.net